William Crawford Williamson

Reminiscences of a Yorkshire Naturalist

William Crawford Williamson

Reminiscences of a Yorkshire Naturalist

ISBN/EAN: 9783337025496

Printed in Europe, USA, Canada, Australia, Japan

Cover: Foto ©Raphael Reischuk / pixelio.de

More available books at **www.hansebooks.com**

REMINISCENCES

OF A

Yorkshire Naturalist

BY THE LATE

WILLIAM CRAWFORD WILLIAMSON
LL.D., F.R.S.

PROFESSOR OF BOTANY IN OWENS COLLEGE, MANCHESTER

EDITED BY

HIS WIFE

LONDON

GEORGE REDWAY

1896

PREFACE

WRITING these reminiscences of his life's work was one of the pleasures of Dr. Williamson's later years. I have thought it better to give them to his readers without alteration, and have done nothing more than put his disconnected sketches into something like order, add a few footnotes, and the last pages.

For kind supervision of the chapter on Palæobotany I am indebted to Dr. D. H. Scott.

I have compiled the list of writings from the "Catalogue of Scientific Works" published by the Royal Society (a proof of the last edition of which —now in the press—was kindly sent me by the Secretary), and from works in my own possession.

A. C. W.

43 ELMS ROAD,
    CLAPHAM COMMON, S.W.

CONTENTS

CHAPTER I

CHAPTER II

CHAPTER III

CHAPTER IV

CHAPTER V

CHAPTER VI

CHAPTER VII

CHAPTER VIII

CHAPTER IX

CHAPTER X

CHAPTER XI

CHAPTER XII

CHAPTER XIII

CHAPTER XIV

BIBLIOGRAPHY

REMINISCENCES OF A
YORKSHIRE NATURALIST

CHAPTER I

John Williamson's narrative—Maternal grandparents—
Crawford laboratory — Childhood — Dame schools —
Mr. Potter's school — Lebberston — Mrs. Johnson —
William Smith—Thomas Hinderwell—Phillips' "Geo-
logy of the Yorkshire Coast "—Smith's personality—
Thornton school—Journey to France—Life at Bour-
bourg.

THE early history of the families of British crafts-
men is rarely preserved, and the only record of my
paternal ancestry is a brief autobiographical memo-
randum, given to me by my father many years ago.
In this he says :—

" The only recollection I have of my grandfather
" is that of an old man living in a small cottage in the
" village of Fridaythorpe, in East Yorkshire, where
" I was once taken by my father to see him.

" My father was shepherd to some of the large
" sheep-farmers in the same district. He was a

A

" hard-working, saving man, who took little pleasure
" beyond a visit to York about once a year.

" The village inn at Fridaythorpe was a place
" where he often met his acquaintance during the
" winter evenings. It was kept by a friend, whom
" he had at various times assisted, by lending him
" money. This man, finding that he could not con-
" duct the house any longer with profit, offered it
" to my father, who was persuaded by his friends
" to take it. This new business required him to be
"more frequently absent from home. Amongst
" other places where he was in the habit of going
" was Driffield. There he became acquainted with,
" and eventually married, Mary Bean. Her father
" was a large market-gardener at Brompton, near
"Scarborough, and he attended the Scarborough
" markets three times a week. My father and
" mother lived at the inn at Fridaythorpe, where I
" was born in the year 1784. They carried it on for
" several years, but finding it did not answer, they
" gave it up, and removed to Scarborough. At that
" time my uncle, William Bean, had established a
" large fruit garden at Scarborough, which he also
" threw open as Subscription Promenade Grounds
" for summer visitors, by whom it was much
" frequented.*

* These gardens occupied the entire space between
Huntriss Row and the present railway station. Their
extent and position are well shown in a map published in
Hinderwell's " History of Scarborough."—A. C. W.

"When about nine years old I was sent into
" these gardens, and when I had been there about
" two years I was apprenticed to my uncle for seven
" years more. Before this time expired my uncle
" died, and it fell to my lot to conduct the business
" until I was eighteen or nineteen years of age. At
" this age, wishing to learn the higher branches of
" gardening, I left the place and took a situation as
" under-gardener at Wykeham Abbey, then in the
" hands of the Langleys. After being at Wykeham
" three years, I became head-gardener to Lord
" Mulgrave, of Mulgrave Castle, near Whitby, where
" I remained several years. When I returned to
" Scarborough I engaged myself to my cousin,
" William Bean, who had carried on his father's
" business since I left for Wykeham. He did not
" like the work of superintendence, and transferred
" it to my shoulders, but soon gave up the gardens
" entirely. I then started business on my own
" account, looking after the gardens of several
" residents of Scarborough, which kept me nicely
" employed.

"It was during my leisure hours at this time that
" I commenced the study of geology, entomology,
" conchology, and ornithology. The collections
" which I made were afterwards deposited in the
" Scarborough Museum, which was built in the year
" 1827–28. To this museum I was appointed curator,
" and fulfilled the duties of the situation more than
" twenty-seven years."

Such is my father's account of himself. The registers kept in and for the parish of Fridaythorpe, his native village, record, " John, son of William " Williamson, baptized September 5th, 1784."

Thus far I have said nothing of my mother and her family. Whilst at Mulgrave my father became engaged to, and afterwards married, Miss Elizabeth Crawford, eldest of the thirteen children of a jeweller and lapidary of Scarborough.

My father's love-making was characteristic of the boundless energy of his later life.

Mulgrave was about twenty-two miles from Scarborough, and his only chance for seeing his betrothed was on Sundays. After he had finished work at the gardens on Saturday night he walked to Scarborough, spent Sunday with my mother, walked back on Sunday night, and was at his post looking after his men at six o'clock on Monday morning.

My maternal grandfather was a Scotchman, born in 1756, and, so far as I can learn, was the son of either a farmer or a small jeweller and watchmaker, living at Haddington: subsequent events make the latter occupation most probable.

At that time Scotland was suffering reaction from the events of "'45." The dominant military party consisted chiefly of English or Irish men, whose officers were proud and overbearing.

My grandfather walking one evening with a friend, whom I very well remember, met two officers, who insisted upon keeping the wall, though they were on the wrong side ; finding the lads disinclined to yield at command, which they had predetermined not to do, one of the officers struck my grandfather with his cane. In response the assailant received a skilful blow, which promptly levelled him with the ground.

Reflection soon showed the young athletes that in the then despotic state of military feeling, serious consequences might ensue. Hence, the same night, they fled across the border, and ultimately reached Whitby.

My grandfather at once obtained work in a watch-maker and jeweller's shop; which inclines one to believe that a part of his Scotch training had been in a similar establishment. A young farmer's daughter, who rode on horseback past his window, on her way to Whitby every market-day, attracted his attention, and he ultimately married her, the lady bringing him at the same time a thousand pounds. The young couple soon came to Scarborough, where my grandfather established himself, and of their thirteen children my mother was the eldest.

My own affection for this fine Scotchman when I was a very young child was intense. One part of his business was the cleaning of clocks, and when he had such duties to perform at the farm-houses of villages surrounding the town, he would take me along with him, bird-nesting by the way dividing the time with clock cleaning. One of this old gentleman's accomplishments was the art of enamelling in gold leaf upon glass ; this he did very beautifully, but by a secret method lost at his death. The son, Walton Crawford, who succeeded to his father's business, also developed a special art, and made peculiar butterfly brooches from local stones.

I was for years in the habit of spending much time in their workshops, watching them cutting and working with the diamond and emery wheels the various agates then obtained abundantly amongst the gravels of the coast, and manufacturing them into pins, bracelets, brooches, and other personal ornaments—a youthful training which became of the utmost value to me more than a third of a century later, when scientific research required me to devote much of my own time to similar work. My eldest brother died of meningitis, in all probability from over-education at too early an age. My father, having himself enjoyed no educational advantages, determined that any child he might have should start life under less difficult conditions ; but unfortunately he knew nothing of the dangers attending the over-stimulation of an infantile brain. The child in question, when under six years of age, being accidentally taken into a friend's printing-office, and seeing a frame of type prepared for printing part of a small newspaper, astonished those who were with him by reading the type, notwithstanding its reversed position. No wonder the child died when little more than five years old.

I was myself born in Huntriss Row, on November 24th, 1816. At this time Bean's Subscription Gardens no longer existed, large plots having been cut off for building purposes. My father had extended his scientific explorations, so as to include in his collection a large number of fossils, minerals, shells, crustaceans, and insects ; in consequence a wing was added to the back of the house, with the object of supplying a spacious room for a museum, wherein to preserve the rapidly increasing store of natural objects. A small room next to this museum witnessed my birth. My only sister Ellen, born in 1813, was then living. At the age of about three years I was sent to my first school. At that time one of the older relics of the town, known as St. Thomas' Hospital, was in existence. It was a small pile of low, white, thatched cottages. In one of these an aged woman and her daughter kept a dame's school,*

* Dr. Williamson has often described his reading lessons; one especially interested him. On a bright spring morning, when the sun streamed through the cottage window and almost extinguished a smouldering fire, the dame, an old lady wearing a frilled cap, sat in an armchair knitting; the student, an eager, white-faced lad, with scarlet frock and white pinafore, stood at her knee, holding a folio some six inches square, called a battledore, on the inside of which the alphabet was printed ; capital letters on one side, small ones on the other. The dame, almost asleep, but mechanically knitting, droned " Large ' A,' Willie," and Willie, with eyes anywhere except on the letter, repeated. " Small ' A,' Willie," droned the sleepy voice. Willie again

and here they inducted me into the mysteries of the alphabet. A few months before this a second brother had been born; he also succumbed to meningitis in July 1822, at the age of three years and nine months. Meanwhile, I was removed to a more advanced dame school, kept for many years in Newborough Street, near the Bar, by one, Miss Bulmer. Later, I was once more removed, this time to a school in which a Miss Doughty wielded the ferule.

About the time of my second brother's death, at the age of five or six years, I was transferred to the school of Mr. William Potter, located for a time at the lower end of Huntriss Row, and later in King Street. At this latter place, where the sons of many of the West Riding middle-class people received their education, I remained a number of years. It cannot be justly affirmed that this school was a bad example of the type to which it belonged; but seeing that the payment for its advantages to day scholars amounted to only one guinea per quarter, the type was not a high one. The usher was rarely a competent man, and the educational system of the period allowed him to be rather a hearer of lessons than a true teacher. There was no pretence of either French or German being taught in schools of this class. Of English grammar,

repeated, when a butterfly, the first of the season, caught his eye, and the young naturalist, regardless alike of dame and letters, darted after it.

I only remember having three lessons out of Lindley Murray. This being replaced by the Eton Latin grammar, over which I had to toil in memoritory fashion; learning in some confused and blundering way to apply its rules to Eutropius, Cæsar, Horace, and Virgil, but knowing very little about the matter, either then or for long afterwards.

On the death of my second brother in the summer of 1822, from the same cerebral disease as had caused the death of his predecessor, Dr. Thompson, an able physician as well as an enthusiastic devotee to the rod, warned my parents that I must be taken away from school, or I should break down in the same manner. Hence the first of many interruptions which reduced my school career almost to a dead letter. I was sent to the farmhouse of a friend who resided at Lebberston, about five miles from Scarborough. Here, during the days of my holiday, I scampered among the haycocks, jumped over corn sheaves, followed the waggons to and from the field, and only returned to my home and school as the summer drew to a close.

An old widow lady named Johnson resided in my father's house, upon whom the domestic care of us children devolved. When the old lady died, she left a few hundreds of pounds to my father, which ought to have helped us; but, unfortunately, through his life he hankered after speculation in shipping, and whenever he found himself in possession of money, indulged this inclination. So, in this instance, the new bequest made him part owner of a brig called "Mercury," which, a few years after, ended her own career, and the chief part of his investment among the rocks south of the Scarborough Spa.

Meanwhile my school life was a succession of broken attendances, alternating with longer or shorter holidays. Each midsummer vacation was ushered in by public recitations, the preparation for which seriously interfered with scholastic work during the greater part of June. On these occasions I became familiar with Home's Tragedy of "Douglas," "The King and the Miller of Mansfield," and somewhat later with Scott's "Lady of the "Lake."

After each of these performances, several weeks were regularly spent at Lebberston. Instructions, I doubt not, were given to Mr. Smith, the farmer, to keep me in the open air as much as possible. Hence he gave me to understand that I was entrusted with a special office connected with the well-being of the farm. I was furnished with a tin canister containing gravel, and it was my duty to wander round the cornfields rattling my canister, in order to frighten away the birds, and prevent them from consuming the grain. Many of these lonely hours were spent in the indulgence of vague dreams, characteristic of the boyish ambition for being "somebody." Now, I was Norval, the Lord of Douglas ; dock stalks supplied me with swords, my straw hat became a shield; and with this armament,. in the combination of heroic solitary declamation with the rattling of my canister, days passed healthily away, but I was unmistakably ambitious of being a hero.

In 1824 my father became personally acquainted with the great Father of Geology, William Smith, and with his subsequently distinguished nephew, the late Professor John Phillips.

In 1826 Dr. Smith and his eccentric wife established themselves in our house, where they dwelt for a considerable time. In the same year my father became friend and correspondent of the late Sir Roderick Murchison, whom Dr. Smith and he conducted on a geological excursion to the more important localities of the Yorkshire coast, with which my father was so thoroughly acquainted. In 1825 Thomas Hinderwell, the distinguished historian of Scarborough, died, leaving a small collection of fossils and minerals to his nephew, William Thornton Duesberry, then a Scarborough solicitor, who offered to give them to the town whenever it should erect an appropriate museum for their reception. Stimulated by this offer, steps were immediately taken for the erection of the present museum, my father at once appointed curator, and a literary and philosophical society was established in connection with it. One equally important event to me was the publication, by Professor Phillips, then curator of the museum at York, of his classic volume on the

"Geology of the Yorkshire Coast." Up to this time
my father's collection of fossils was practically un-
named, but the appearance of Phillips' book, in
which most of our specimens were figured, enabled
us to remedy this defect. Every evening was devoted
by us to accomplishing the work. This was my first
introduction to true scientific study. I had long
before accompanied my father on his geological
excursions, and about the same time we worked
together forming collections of the coleoptera and
lepidoptera of North-Eastern Yorkshire; but exact
scientific palæontological nomenclature had not previously constituted any part of my study. We had
hitherto had nothing to guide us beyond the unscientific volume of Young and Bird on the "Geology
of the Yorkshire Coast." Phillips' accurate volume
initiated an entirely new order of things. Many a
time did I mourn over the publication of this book,
and the consequences immediately resulting from it.
Instead of indulging in the games and idleness to
which most lads are prone, my evenings throughout
a long winter were devoted to the detested labour of
naming these miserable stones. Such is the short-
sightedness of boyhood. Pursuing this uncongenial
work gave me in my thirteenth year a thorough
practical familiarity with the palæontological treasures of Eastern Yorkshire. This early acquisition
happily moulded the entire course of my future
life.

One of the grandest figures that ever frequented

Eastern Yorkshire was William Smith, the distinguished Father of English Geology. My boyish
reminiscence of the old engineer, as he sketched a
triangle on the flags of our yard, and taught me how
to measure it, is very vivid. The drab knee-
breeches and grey worsted stockings, the deep waist-
coat, with its pockets well furnished with snuff—of
which ample quantities continually disappeared within
the finely chiselled nostril—and the dark coat with its
rounded outline and somewhat quakerish cut, are all
clearly present to my memory.

Spending the greater portion of his morning in
writing, towards noon he would slowly wend his way
to the museum, where he always found in my father
a friend with whom to gossip about the rocks of the
Cotswolds, the clays of Kimmeredge, or the drainage
of the Eastern Fens. He would expound in a
Coleridgean fashion his ideas of their relation to
the strata of Yorkshire and of the other parts of
England. His walking pace never varied; it was slow
and dignified; he was usually followed a few yards
in the rear by his rose-cheeked partner in life. We
have a thousand times contemplated the fine old man,
who, amid his favourite haunts, thus laid the foundations of geological science.

Smith's memory was most remarkable, especially
in anything relative to his own life. On the occasion
already referred to, when he and my father took Sir
Roderick and Lady Murchison along the Yorkshire
coast they parted company at Saltburn, the

Murchisons proceeding towards Brora in Scotland, where he had property on which he suspected the Oolitic strata existed, and for the investigation of which the practical lesson he had just received was a valuable preparation. Smith and my father returned on foot to Whitby, chatting very freely by the way. They had traversed many miles of picturesque and ever varying road, when they reached a point where it was about to make a small curve. They had already passed several similar ones, but on reaching the point in question, Smith said to my father: " It is now twenty-eight years " since I came along this road, but if I rightly " remember, when we turn that corner, we shall " see a small bridge over a brook." The words were scarcely out of his mouth, when the two were standing upon the bridge, with the brook brawling beneath their feet.

The early part of the year 1831 was spent at Thornton, near Pickering, with the Rev. Thomas Irving, master of the small village grammar school. This was to me a delightful time. I made my way thither along with the son of a Scarborough tradesman who was already a pupil in the school, and our journey was characteristic, alike of the inexperience of boyhood and the lack of principle in stage coach officials. We travelled from Scarborough to Stainton, a distance of ten miles, by the York mail, on leaving which the guard came to me for the perquisite, customary in those days. In my ignorance, this being my first independent journey, though we had travelled only a single stage, instead of giving him the wonted sixpence, I felt it my duty to give, as he felt it his duty to take, and from a young, inexperienced lad, half a crown. But this was not our only folly ; we had to walk the five miles intervening between Stainton and Thornton, where tea would be awaiting us. But were we not on a journey, and did we not think it fine to do as we had heard of other travellers doing ? *ergo,* we ordered tea to be prepared for us in the inn before starting on our walk. No tea we ever tasted was so delicious as this, which we ordered and paid for ourselves. Needing the tea or no was not any consideration, the luxury of being our own masters constituted the charm, though it cleared our pocket money.

On entering upon the school work, I found myself in an unwonted atmosphere. Hitherto, I, along with my class, had been accustomed to prepare sixty or seventy lines of Virgil within the space of an hour. The thing was not to be done by young, imperfectly taught lads. I had looked forward with dread to my first Latin task in the new school. This was soon given, and consisted of three lines of the "Æneid." I could not comprehend the meaning of so pleasant a change, but this meaning became clear when the class stood round Mr. Irving's desk. We were expected to understand, not only every word, but every syllable or letter of both the syntax and the prosody in those three lines. This was a revelation to me of what true teaching meant, and at a later period the loss of it cost me many a tearful night. Two things in the history of that brief school-life are worth recording. We were entitled to two half holidays each week, but not on any fixed day. Hence, if a day was unusually fine we had only to ask, in order to have either the ordinary half-day or both halves rolled into one glorious whole. In such cases boys and ushers alike rejoiced in the rambles to distant woods and moors. These rambles in that lovely limestone region were indeed pleasures. I had brought to the school all nets and other entomological apparatus for increasing the museum collection of British insects, in which the district around Thornton was remarkably rich. A taste for such pursuits spread rapidly amongst the boys, and insect hunting soon became the popular occupation whenever we were free, even if for only half an hour.

This happy time came to an end all too soon. At the close of June I returned to Scarborough, and then began another of the numerous breaks in my scholastic career. This lasted until the end of September, and the three months were again spent in collecting plants, birds, and fossils for the museum.

My parents determined to send me next for a while into France; and having heard that the son of a Leeds merchant whose acquaintance my father had made, was at a school in Bourbourg, a small town north-east of Calais, they decided I should also go. What followed is characteristic of two things not uncommon in those pre-railroad times— viz., lack of experience in travel; and along with costly postage a very considerable lack of cash. One of my mother's brothers occupied a responsible position in a merchant's warehouse which stood in Cheapside, at the corner of Wood Street, and my first business was to find my way to him. I had never before been more than twenty miles away from home. Under these circumstances, it would have been reasonable for my parents to have ascertained that my uncle was at home and could receive me, instead of pitching a raw young lad into the heart of London alone. The steamer "James Watt," running between Leith and London, picked me up at Scarborough on the afternoon of the last Sunday in September 1831, and landed me at Blackwall early on Tuesday morning. I had then to reach London, a distance of several miles, and, knowing nothing of omnibuses or cabs, I stepped into the first vehicle I found on the Quay, which was a two-horse hackney coach, for which I had to pay seven-and-sixpence out of my thinly lined purse. On reaching my uncle's warehouse I received the paralysing information that he was in Scotland, and would not be home for some days. The steamer which was to convey me cheaply to Calais sailed from the Thames a little after noon, and meanwhile I had to go to the French Ambassador's office in order to obtain a passport. The kind head of the firm with which my uncle was connected instructed me where to go to obtain this indispensable document. Following his direction, I found myself face to face with the French officials, who speedily informed me no passport could be granted to a lad like me, unless some older person was with me when making the application.

I told them I could not wait, that I was leaving London by the steamer which sailed in an hour or two, but all in vain; they were inexorable, and I had to make my way back to Cheapside, and inform my new friend of the failure of my mission. He then kindly accompanied me to the Passport Office, where my eyes, nose, mouth, and eyebrows were duly described on the stamped document which I then received. But meanwhile the steamer had sailed. I well remember my kind companion bringing me back to Cheapside, by a way which enabled me to see the celebrated Covent Garden Market, but on reaching his warehouse the important question arose, what was to be done? No other packet sailed from London to Calais until the succeeding Friday. Meanwhile the merchant recommended me to take up my quarters at the well-known coaching house, the "Cross Keys" in Wood Street, just opposite the end of his own warehouse. I took possession of a poor but inexpensive attic and proceeded to review the situation. I soon arrived at the conclusion that my slender stock of

money would have entirely disappeared before
Friday, leaving nothing wherewith to reach Calais
and Bourbourg.

Wretched beyond measure, and not knowing what
to do, I threw myself down upon my bed, and then
recollected having heard that when in trouble
nothing afforded such consolation as reading the
Bible! I at once extracted from my trunk one
which my mother had put there, and proceeded to
try the experiment; with what result I cannot say.
One thing, however, became clear to me, I must
find some quicker way of reaching Calais than
waiting for Friday's steamer. The landlord of the
"Cross Keys" was called into consultation, and I learnt
from him that a coach started from his office, at eight
o'clock that evening, which would reach Dover early
next morning. This was a much more costly route
than the one by which I had intended to go, but
there was no other way open to me that would not
cost more still. In due time I was mounted on the
top of the coach, which had scarcely cleared the
suburbs of London when heavy rain began to fall,
and long before we reached Canterbury I was soaked
to the skin. We had a short delay at the posting
house at that place, where we hoped to enjoy the
luxury of hot coffee. But everywhere the fates
pursued. We entered the inn only to find the
waiting woman had overslept herself, and was at
that moment applying a match to a large black coal
fire, which altogether declined to be lighted, whilst

we remained shivering in the cold. We returned to our conveyance more starved than when we had descended from it, and terminated a wet and miserable journey only on reaching Dover.

Then, and for many a long year afterwards, my highest ambition was for the time to arrive when I could afford to travel inside a stage coach.

The journey from Calais to Bourbourg, a distance of fourteen or fifteen miles, had to be taken by cabriolet, a jingling one-horse vehicle. When about half way I saw near the road side a cabaret, whose sign announced that "Vin Ordinaire" was to be had within. Now, I had never tasted this notorious beverage, and thought I should like to do so. I therefore gave my cocher a franc, and told him to bring me as much as the coin would buy. To my astonishment he produced a huge jugful, the tenth part of which sufficed to satisfy my curiosity ; but he speedily disposed of the remainder. I arrived at the house of Monsieur Montieus, my future schoolmaster, about ten o'clock at night. The door was opened by a tall English usher, who of course wanted to know my errand. When I told him this, and that no letter had previously announced my coming, he asked where I was from, and when I gave him this piece of information he was still more astonished, discovering as he did that my parents lived within a few miles of his own Yorkshire home. Monsieur Montieus was summoned, and at once announced to me there was no vacancy in his school—a fresh addition to my

youthful disasters. But he proposed sending me to
his father, the Abbe Montieus, who had a school some
hundred miles south of Bourbourg. Unfortunately,
I not only had no money left to pay the expense of
so long a journey, but I had been compelled to spend
ten shillings entrusted to me by friends of the Leeds
boy. The case appeared desperate, but it was at
last concluded I must remain where I was until my
parents could be communicated with. I was, however, presently told a vacancy could be found for me
as parlour boarder, a sort of extra respectable
class, which dined at a small table in the centre of
the *salle à manger*, whilst the other boys were
seated at tables ranged round the walls of the room.
This upper crust had also the privilege of remaining
in the salon on Sundays for dessert and French
wine after the other boys had departed. To all
this, however, although considerable extra fees
were to be paid, my parents unfortunately consented.

I soon found I was practically in an English school
in France. Madame Montieus was an excellent
English lady, the usher was the son of a Yorkshire
farmer, and we had more English boys than French.
Though a nominal fine was imposed upon every lad
caught speaking other than French, we really
talked little else than English. Sending English lads
to learn French at schools of this type was common
then, and may be so still. I can only marvel that
any parents with a modicum of worldly wisdom

would do so. Had I been forwarded to the school
of the Abbe Montieus all had been well, I might then
have learnt some French; as it was, I learnt nothing.
Even the classical teaching was as different as possible from that which a few months previously had
stimulated my efforts at the Thornton school. I
felt I was losing instead of gaining ground, and night
after night, miserable and disheartened, I wept myself
to sleep.

A short experience showed me the social life of
the school was domineered by a bully of a lad from
Leeds, not the one for whom I should have brought ten
shillings. Any boy who incurred the displeasure of
this lad was at once by him cut off from intercourse
with the rest of the school, and remained so until he
chose to lift the ban. At first, two unfortunate
coloured lads from the West Indies fell victims to
this overbearing conduct. Then I and the only lad of
any social position in the school, the son of one of
the great London municipal families, fell under the
tyrant's displeasure and were treated accordingly.
We were for months cut off from our fellows, indeed
until the day I left Bourbourg. How great the fear
of this terrible lad had been, may be judged from the
fact, that during all this time no one dared to acquaint
Monsieur Montieus with what was going on. When,
however, he, one of the very kindest of men, learned
the state of things, the tyrant was deposed in disgrace.

My own woeful experiences of a Continental school
induces me to give a word of warning to parents who

even in this day, would send their children abroad, to ascertain very fully the kind of establishment to which they entrust the young ones. I left France, having learnt little more of colloquial French than I brought with me, and not having gained any compensating advantage.

CHAPTER II

AT the end of March 1832 I returned home.
Instructions had, however, been sent to me to
spend a few days in London, and especially to call
upon my father's old friend, Sir Roderick Murchison,
the distinguished geologist. This was to me a
solemn business. Murchison, Sedgwick, Lyell,
and Buckland were the deities of my geological
Olympus. When, having been invited to breakfast
with the great man, I stood upon his doorstep in
Bryanston Place, I had scarcely courage to ring
the door bell.

I was, however, received in the kindest manner by my host and hostess. Lady Murchison was indeed one of the most charming of women, and her kindness to me on that occasion has been vividly remembered ever since. Sir Roderick took me down to the Museum of the Geological Society, then in Somerset House; I was there introduced to that excellent geologist, Mr. Lonsdale, then curator of the museum and assistant secretary of the Society. Many interesting things were shown to me, especially a remarkable fossil, brought by Murchison from Oehningen in Switzerland, well known to me as the fossil fox. The identification of such fossils in those days was not very exact, but having had at home representations of this specimen, which my father had received from its discoverer, along with a lithograph made from a sketch by Lady Murchison, of the Alpine valley in which it was found, I stood enchanted when the original creature, so often the subject of my geological ponderings, was actually in my hands.

Another event of my young life was an acquaintance with some of the London theatres. I had been from earliest childhood trained to an appreciation of fine acting; indeed, several members of my mother's family were amateur dramatic artists of no mean order. In Scarborough I had seen Charles Young as Hamlet, the elder Kean as Richard III., Charles Kemble as the Hunchback, and Braham as Tom Bowling. I now saw Liston as Paul Pry, Fanny Kemble in "Francis First," Madame Taglioni in

" The Shadow Dance," and Madame Vestris in " The Cork Leg."

I heard Lablache sing " L'Elixir d'Amour," and lastly, I saw O'Keefe in " High Life Below Stairs."*

On reaching home, I found arrangements had been made to place me as medical student with Mr. Thomas Weddell, a rising general practitioner in Scarborough. The direct results of this arrangement were of a varied character, some good, others the reverse. But several events occurred during the three years I occupied that position which materially influenced my future life.

Meanwhile the general circumstances of students destined for the medical profession in provincial towns were, at the beginning of the century, so different from anything existing now, that I propose to put some of these conditions on record, if only to show to medical students now living how great are the advantages which they enjoy, compared with those of their representatives of half a century ago.

On being transferred to this new sphere, I found an older student of the name of Hopper, son of the proprietor of the well-known Bell Hotel of the town.

The day on which I entered upon my duties was significant of what was to follow. A considerable part of the day was spent at a big pestle and

---

* Dr.Williamson enjoyed to within six months of his death describing these scenes. To his mind no danseuse equalled these old ones, and not even Toole's Paul Pry was quite equal to the one he knew.—A. C. W.

mortar with which divers medicaments had to be
hammered and brayed, until the bulk could be
passed through a fine hair sieve. Then came preparations of certain infusions, in which senna leaves,
gentian roots, rose leaves, etc., had severally to be
put into jugs, which were filled with boiling water and
tightly closed.

During the day the Governor, as I found Mr.
Weddell was always designated, occasionally called
at the surgery to order medicines that happened to
be wanted immediately. But the great time for
work began about six o'clock in the evening, when
the physic-making for the day took place. At that
time few patients, excepting such as lived in the
country, and whose visits involved the hire of a
horse, paid for anything beyond the cost of medicines which they received. Payment for visits was
almost unknown among second-rate general practitioners in provincial towns.

Such practitioners were paid for their services by
the sale of drugs, which their patients must swallow.
As my governor had a very large practice among the
middle and lower classes of a maritime fishing town
such as Scarborough then was, the number of
draughts and mixtures to be compounded, pills to
be rolled, ointments to be rubbed up, and blisters
and plasters to be spread, made the two or three
hours after six o'clock a busy time. Even when all
this was accomplished, the day's work was not done.
On my first evening I had to accompany the senior

pupil on a tour round the town, when we distributed these said medicines to the houses of the several patients for whom they were destined—a journey from which we returned only as the clock struck ten. I then learnt another fact : our governor was a bachelor, whose only servant was also practically housekeeper, and lived in a large, comfortable cellar kitchen. We pupils took breakfast, dinner, and tea in the dining-room along with the governor ; but on our return from the physic-distributing tour, I found the evenings, all work finished, were to be spent in the kitchen with our housekeeper-servant. Our bedroom was an attic at the top of the house; so far as sleeping was concerned, comfortable enough, but when morning dawned, new social lights dawned also. Our attic contained no provision whatever of the lavatory kind; for the performance of all such functions we must descend to a brick-floored cellar in the basement of the house and behind the kitchen, where not only our toilet was performed, but where, in addition, I found we had to clean our own boots. We had also, before breakfast, to sweep the surgery floor.

The second day was pretty much a repetition of the first, save that my journey of the previous evening was supposed to have made me familiar with the addresses of all the patients ; hence I was installed in the honourable office of errand boy, vice Hopper resigned.

The house had two sitting-rooms—one behind the other. An outside covered passage ran alongside these

parlours and led to an area, partly yard, partly
garden behind, in which was the so-called surgery.
Halfway up this passage was the kitchen entrance,
over which an oil lamp hung from the ceiling, though
this was the only lobby lamp of the house; because
the way to the surgery passed under it, the care
and trimming of this oil lamp was deemed another
of the varied duties of the " medical student." The
arrival of Saturday revealed a further extension of
those duties. All the bottles, jars, and other recep-
tacles of drugs were to be taken down, cleaned, and,
if need be, refilled, and the shelves dusted; whilst
the last duty at night, after clearing away all dis-
orderly indications of the day's work, was to rub the
top of the counter with beeswax and turpentine, that
it might present a shining face on the Sabbath. This
Saturday evening duty was fulfilled by me weekly,
without omission, during the whole of the three years
in which I occupied my position in the surgery.

Though essentially an errand boy, I did not carry
the traditional " basket ; " hence coats with a superabundance of sportsmen's pockets were a necessary
portion of our outfit. But this arrangement was not
wholly satisfactory ; it had its dangers. Not unfrequently the young folks of both sexes familiar
with our duties contrived, by well-timed "accidents,"
as we went on our way, roughly to jostle us, in the
not always futile hope of smashing one of the physic
bottles with which these pockets were known to be
stuffed. A second difficulty not unfrequently sprang

from this plan : from time to time the ringing of the surgery bell whilst I was enjoying my supper and rest announced that some small box of pills, or packet of powders, promised by the governor to a patient had not arrived. It had probably lurked, over-looked, at the bottom of one of my many capacious pockets. Occasionally the omitted delivery was not discovered until the governor made his professional visit the succeeding day. On his return to the sur-gery, a frowning brow indicated thunder in the air, and the explosion usually took the shape of "H'm ! "At your old trade of basket-making, sir ?" I heard the phrase too often not at once to feel my various pockets in search of the missing powder or bolus.

The middle of November brought fresh work. On St. Martin's Day domestic and farm servants in the east of Yorkshire not unfrequently changed their situations ; and as we had a considerable number of patients in this class, we were obliged to be careful their "bills" were delivered before they left their temporary home and were lost sight of by us for ever.

This November bill-work was, however, but the pilot-balloon of what had to be undertaken during December. In those days the length of a doctor's bill was proverbial. Nowadays the patient receives from his doctor a polite note intimating "the amount due for professional attendance," and as the greater part even of this brief communication is elegantly

lithographed, the business of making out the Christmas bills is easily performed.

It was seriously otherwise in my day. The ledger
account recorded every pill, powder, or other healing
medicament that had been delivered to the patient
during the entire year; hence, when the household
was both large and sickly, the length of the bill was
literally a great one. But length was not the only
evil for us poor students. After adding half a
column of minute items, the result as shown by the
bill did not always correspond with those given in
the ledger. In these cases the whole affair had to
be overhauled, to learn where and why the dis-
crepancy existed; and as this happened probably in
one long bill out of every three, the toil thus superadded was no joke.

But when this labour was successfully accomplished, and every bill lay neatly folded, the end was
not fulfilled. Even the distribution of these yearly
accounts devolved upon the junior pupil. The town
bills easily reached their destination, but the country
ones were a graver consideration. They involved
two journeys, each of a day, on horseback. Unfortunately, I was no equestrian, and so journeyed
from village to village, wondering as I went, how
long it would be before my horse and its rider took
different views of their respective duties. At last the
question was settled. As I was leaving the village
of Seamer at nightfall, on my way to Aytoun, my
steed pitched me over his head, and stood quietly

and contemptuously gazing at me as I lay on my
back in the mud. Many of the duties which I have
referred to, and which ought chiefly to have been
performed by an errand-boy, are easily explained
when the time and circumstances are remembered.

Mr. Weddell had originally been chemist and
druggist, and entered the profession when the
Apothecaries' Act of 1815 afforded facilities for men
in similar positions to become regular practitioners.

He, and all such, brought with them into their new
position ideas associated with the system of apprenticeship to retail trades in shops. Lads thus apprenticed must of course perform these menial tasks, and
time was required to bring about a more enlightened
arrangement, suitable to the better educated youths
who entered the medical profession at later periods.

Still, although we learnt little of our profession
that could not have been mastered in a few weeks
spent in an apothecary's shop, the three years of
"medical studentship" in Scarborough were not
without redeeming features, in the abundant open-
air exercise which I was partly compelled, partly
permitted, to take. During the spring and summer
months the coast north of Scarborough was frequented by various sandpipers and other wading
and aquatic birds. The North Bay itself was
then a much more retired nook than it now is.
The construction of the pier and the stone embankment have drawn away many of the birds, then so
much more abundant than they now are. We were

frequently out with our guns at dawn, and many
valuable birds still in the museum at Scarborough
were obtained during these early rambles.   On
other occasions we were plant-hunting.   I was then
forming a collection of the plants of Eastern Yorkshire, as well as trying to master the natural
classification which was already beginning to
supplant the Linnæan method, so long the one
universally adopted.

Many of our best collecting grounds were at a
distance, and we often started on our journey
before daybreak; in this a little practical difficulty had to be overcome.   Having frequently a
companion on these excursions, we were not always
able to leave our beds simultaneously.   For this we
invented a remedy; each of us provided a long
string, one end of which was tied round the
sleeper's wrist, whilst the other was flung out of the
window, and could be reached by any person outside ; thus the first to rise was able to arouse his
companion.   From time to time the ludicrous side of
our arrangement became manifest.   When neither
of us awoke at the time arranged for, these strings
hung down the front of our respective houses
until the servants of the neighbourhood were on the
move ; and they, having become familiar with our
plans, took care vigorously to arouse us.

One of these mornings was to me a somewhat
interesting one.   The nature and functions of the
stamens and pistils of each flowering plant were

then well known to every student, but no one had
yet discovered organs with similar functions in any
of the cryptogamic forms of vegetation, and I was
ambitious of making this discovery. Resting after
a long ramble on the brow of Oliver's Mount, I
found close within my reach a fine tuft of the well-
known moss, Polytrichum commune. On examining
some of these objects with my pocket lens, I discovered at the apex of each stem a lovely little cup,
formed of small coloured leaflets, and which looked
very like minute flowers. I wondered whether or
not the organs so many botanists were in search of
were enclosed within that little cup ; and, indeed, it
was in such a cup they were found years afterwards
by Hoffmeister, Unger, and others, who followed in
their steps. I little dreamed that what I was in
search of was actually under my eyes ; but these
reproductive organs of the cryptogams differ altogether in form and aspect from those of the flowering plant, though functionally identical. The labours
of many men who were led into the right path by
Suminski and Hoffmeister were needed to clear the
mysteries by which the subject was invested.

During the earlier part of my student life I forwarded to the Zoological Society of London a
memoir on the rare birds found in the vicinity of
Scarborough. This was one of the earliest of my
attempts at drawing up a scientific memoir, still,
some of the facts recorded in it were subsequently
referred to by Yarrell in his " History of the

" Birds of Great Britain." But I was soon called to another, a more enduring piece of work. Previous to the third decade of the nineteenth century, very little was known respecting the vegetation of the Oolitic age, but the discovery of a small esturian deposit of plants in Gristhorpe Bay made great additions to our information on this subject. There have always been discussions respecting the share which the two cousins, William Bean and my father, were entitled to claim in this discovery; that the subsequent development of it was pro- secuted chiefly by them is indisputable. In March 1832 the publication of Lindley and Hutton's " Fossil "Flora of Great Britain" was commenced; and shortly afterwards Mr. Dunn, then secretary to the Literary and Philosophical Society of Scarborough, received a letter from Mr. Hutton, inquiring if there was any one in the town capable of figuring and describing the new plants of the Gristhorpe deposit. Mr. Dunn brought this letter to me, and urged me to undertake the task. I did so, and contributed to the pages of that work almost as long as its quarterly parts continued to be issued. At length the issue ceased, because, as Mr. Lindley himself told me, the geologists did not give the work that financial support which he had hoped, whilst he as botanist did not feel called upon to spend his money upon a publication that, after all, was mainly a geological one. So far as my own communications to it are concerned, some of the palæontologists familiar with its pages may be amused to learn that most of my drawings were prepared at one end of Mr. Weddell's kitchen-table, whilst the housekeeper was occupied at the other end with the several processes of providing the day's dinner.

But this was not my only invitation into new botanical work. Mr. Weddell had undertaken to deliver lectures at the Mechanics' Institution on vegetable physiology, and he asked me to prepare for him a set of diagrams illustrating the subject. My own knowledge was then too small to enable me to do this without reading. At that time almost the only popular English book on vegetable physiology was Mrs. Marcett's "Conversations"; hence it was to this elementary publication that I applied myself. The result was the acquisition of a taste which I never subsequently lost.

A short holiday which my father and I devoted to a geological excursion along the coast, between Robin Hood's Bay and Skinningrave, produced also permanent results.

I knew fairly well the general features of the ground over which we proposed to work, as well as Smith's views respecting the identification of each larger group of strata by means of the fossils which it contained.

Observations made during this excursion showed me that Smith's generalisations did not embrace all the facts of the case. Whilst working among the beds of the Upper Lias, which on the York-

shire coast consist of three very distinct superimposed layers, I became convinced that the fossils
characteristic of that stratum were not distributed
indiscriminately throughout its entire thickness.
I found that, though each of these three layers was
well distinguished by its lithological structure, the
distinction became much more marked when we
examined the fossils which each of them contained.
Thus the fossil wood known as Whitby jet, with
which even the Romans were familiar, is obtained
almost wholly from the middlemost of these three
layers, and I observed that many other of the Lias
fossils had their respective zones, in which alone
they were to be found.

Struck with these facts, I proceeded to investigate the coast strata between the Lias and the
Cornbrash, and I found here similar conditions.
I embodied these observations in two papers, which
were read before the Geological Society of London,
one on the Liassic Strata on May 9th, 1834, and
the other on the Oolitic Rocks, November 2nd,
1836. These two memoirs were ultimately united
by the Society, and published in a single memoir in
their " Transactions." We shall, I think, shortly see
why this was done.

Towards the end of 1836, and almost simultaneously with the receipt of my second memoir, a
short but carefully prepared paper by Mr. Louis
Hunton, a hitherto unknown author, was forwarded
to the Society and shortly afterwards read. This

paper was entitled: "Accompanying Remarks to a
"Section of the Upper Lias and Marlstone of York-
"shire, showing the Limited Vertical Range of the
"species of Ammonites and other Testacea, with
"their Value as Geological Tests." This memoir
obviously dealt with part of the series of strata that
had been the subject of my first paper, read two
and a half years previously. The author was
evidently ignorant of my memoir, but he had
arrived at conclusions identical with those which I
had announced in May 1834.

This contribution of Mr. Hunton's was at once
printed, as was my second communication, but
oddly enough the latter was tacked on to the end
of my first paper, which had lain neglected in one
of the Society's pigeon-holes. There is no great
difficulty in realising what must have occurred.
In 1834, either through the influence of the President, or because the Council shared his esti-
mate of the small value of my communication, the
latter was thrown overboard as not deserving to
be published.

When, in 1836 a new observer, ignorant of what
I had done, reported to them the existence of conditions which they had in practice previously refused
to admit on my authority, they now felt obliged
to publish his paper, and doing so compelled them
in common justice to publish mine also. The arrival
of my second paper gave them the opportunity for
this and the separate productions of Hunton and

myself now rest side by side in the same volume of their " Transactions."

In 1876 Messrs. Tate and Blake published their work on the Yorkshire Lias, in which they not only confirmed but considerably extended the conclusions at which I had arrived in 1834. But here again a trivial arrangement on the part of the Geological Society led into an unintentional injustice to me. In printing our memoirs, the Society placed Mr. Hunton's name in front of mine. This seems to have suggested to the two authors the idea of Mr. Hunton's priority. Commenting on our observations on page 6 of their work, they say :

"In 1836, in Vol. V. of the second series of the "'Geological Transactions' were published two " papers ; *the first* by Louis Hunton, 'Accompanying "' Remarks to a Section of the Upper Lias and Marl- "' stone of Yorkshire, showing the Limited Vertical "' range of the species of Ammonites and other "' Testacea, with their value as Geological Tests.' " This paper contains very valuable information " upon a limited portion of the series *and is the* " *first attempt to do* what we have undertaken in the " present work, namely, to localise the fossils in " their various horizons. In the second paper by " W. C. Williamson, ' on the Distribution of Fossil "' Remains on the Yorkshire Coast,' the same work " is attempted for the whole of the Lias, and the more " easily acquired facts are accurately laid down."

Messrs. Tate and Blake thus credit Mr. Hunton

with priority over me, whereas I had, as already
shown, preceded him by two years and a half. My
friend, Professor Judd, now President of the Geological
Society, has suggested to me another and more
kindly explanation of the delay in the publication in
question. In those days fewer papers were published
than now, and the quarto volumes of " Geological
" Transactions " did not appear at regular intervals.
Hence the possibility that my memoirs may have
been read during such an interval between the publication of two volumes and had to wait until the
next was ready for the press.

Still later I applied the same method of investigation to rocks yet higher in the series, viz., the Cornbrash, the Kelloway Rocks, and the Oxford Clay.
This inquiry and its results were embodied in a third
memoir, read on May 9th, 1838, and published in
the " Transactions " shortly afterwards. Subsequent researches have established the fact that very
thin zones of stratified rocks are often identified,
even by the presence of some single fossil, and such
horizontal zones are now recognised as having great
practical value.

During my medical studentship my father and I
acquired considerable knowledge of the Birds and
Insects of Eastern Yorkshire. In the latter branch
of study we had made one fortunate discovery.
We had early collected a single specimen of a
beetle unknown to us, and were unable to learn
the name until we found in Curtis's " British Ento-

"mology," on plate 6, a figure and description of our insect. It proved to be Nebria Livida. The writer stated that an extremely small number—I think three or four isolated examples—had been collected on the Lincolnshire coast. We wholly failed to recollect where we had obtained our single specimen. Long afterwards, we were working amongst the rocks of Cornbrash, which, fallen from a higher part of the precipitous cliff, were then strewn in considerable numbers over the sandy shore of the south-eastern corner of the north bay of Scarborough. Turning over one of these blocks, my eye quickly detected a "Nebria" running out of the depressed sand upon which the stone had rested. Securing my prize, I quickly joined my father, and showed him my captured treasure. We then remembered that this was the place where we had obtained our original specimen. It was long before other localities were discovered from which the insect could be obtained in any numbers; and since it re-appeared at ours every summer, until the bridge and embankment ruined the spot, we were able to supply the needs of our entomological friends.

On another occasion we were out in a boat with a friend to obtain specimens of "Terns" or sea swallows, that were flying in the bay. Whilst thus occupied, we noticed two or three Skua gulls amongst the Terns. Skua gulls are birds that do not catch their own fish, but mingle with others that are doing so; and, when one of the latter has been successful, the Skua immediately gives chase to him, and makes him disgorge his prey, which prey the Skua catches before it reaches the water. But on shooting one of these buccaneers of the sea, they were unable to identify it with any of the known forms of Arctic birds. Further examination, however, showed it to be a new species of the genus now known as Pomerine Skua.

CHAPTER III

ANOTHER branch of study occupied me during my
medical apprenticeship. In the early part of this
century a large amount of attention was being paid
both in Great Britain and Ireland, as well as in
Denmark and other northern parts of Europe, to
antique remains, especially the tumuli, then so abundant. These researches were promoted at home by
Sir Richard Cole Hoare at this early period ; and
later by Canon Greenwell, of Durham. East Yorkshire was particularly rich in these relics of a
bygone age. One fine example of a tumulus or
place of interment had been known to exist on the

margin of Gristhorpe Cliff, overhanging the sea at Gristhorpe Bay, a few miles to the south of Scarborough. On July 10th or 11th, 1834, this tumulus was opened by W. Beswick, Esq., the owner of the property on which it was located. He was accompanied by a few friends, of whom my father was one. Its contents proved to be of the utmost interest. The first object which presented itself to the eyes of the excavators was the trunk of a large oak tree laid horizontally at about six feet from the surface of the ground. On using proper tackle for raising this object, only the upper part of it came away, leaving the lower portion embedded in clay. It now became evident this was the trunk of an oak tree, split lengthwise, and retaining its bark, which, after having been cut down, had been hollowed, converting it into a rude coffin. During his long career as archæologist, Sir Richard Colt Hoare had met with only one similar example in Great Britain, though such coffins are more frequently found in the Scandinavian districts, especially in South Jutland; and others like it were subsequently met with in our own country. Most if not all of these tree interments appear to have belonged to the Bronze Age. The coffin was half filled with water. The embedded portion was now taken up, and its contents carefully removed. The entire collection of objects, coffin included, was ultimately transferred to the Scarborough Museum, to which institution

it was presented by Mr. Beswick. Special attention
was at once given to the bones of the skeleton, which
were in an extremely rotten condition, owing to the
decay and disappearance of the membranous parts,
which when present hold together the calcareous
elements. It was then suggested, probably by Dr.
Harland, one of the most intelligent of the medical
men then residing in the town, that these bones should
be carefully washed and put into a common laundry
boiler filled with a thin solution of glue. This was
done, the fire lit and carefully watched, that the
precious bones should not be injured by any too
violent ebullition. It fell to my lot to undertake this
part of the proceedings. The bones were absolutely black, the effect apparently of the tannic or
gallic acid contained in the bark of the oak tree,
and which had combined with the iron of the clay in
which the coffin was embedded.

The process of boiling was continued for about
eight hours, after which the bones were carefully exposed to the air, to allow the gelatine to harden. After
this, they were articulated as readily as recent bones
could have been. The original owner of these bones
proved to have been a fellow about six feet in height;
that he was an old man was indicated by the advanced
ossification of some of the cartilages of the skeleton,
and by the surfaces of his teeth being worn away to
an almost uniform flatness; in all other respects the
teeth were in a state of perfect preservation; the

old fellow had obviously never needed the services
of a dentist. Amongst other objects found in the
coffin were a bronze spearhead, three flints, and two
beautifully worked bone objects. One of these was
a pin, and the other apparently part of the handle
of a dagger or knife, which had evidently been
fastened to the end of a wooden shaft by three pins,
which had passed completely through both the bone
and the wood.

Soon after this discovery was made, it was
intimated to me by some of my friends that it was
my duty to write an illustrated account of the matter.
This I did to the best of my power, though the under-
taking of such a task by a youth, who had not yet
reached his eighteenth year, was rather appalling.
However, the thing was done, and the memoir
published at Scarborough before the end of the year.
It happened that shortly after this pamphlet appeared
the late Professor Buckland paid a visit to the town
and obtained a copy of the memoir, with which he
seemed to be much pleased; but I heard no more of
the matter until the weekly issue of the *Literary
Gazette* for October 18th, 1834, was forwarded to
me by some unknown hand. On opening the
number I found that, unlike its usual form, nearly an
entire half had been devoted to the recapitulation of
part of my archæological bantling, and the number
for the succeeding week contained the repro-
duction, in like manner, of the remaining half.
No mention was made of how it reached the editor's ·

hands, beyond some associated observations and allusions to my youthful geological pursuits. These caused me to write to the great Oxford Professor, thanking him for his kind action. At that time many of my contributions had been published in Lindley and Hutton's " Fossil Flora," and I presume he had these in his mind when, in a letter replying to mine, he said: " I was much gratified at seeing that the " editor of the *Literary Gazette* took the same view " that I had done of your interesting account of " the British tumulus, and am happy to have " been instrumental in bringing before the public a " name to which I look forward as likely to figure in " the annals of British science. I trust you will not " fail to receive in your native town that encourage- " ment which strangers, so far as their means extend, " are ready to proffer to you." It may readily be conceived how great an impression the receipt of a communication like this, from so eminent a man, would make upon its youthful recipient. I can, how- ever, distinctly remember that it did not feed my vanity half so much as it aroused within me a deep yet encouraging sense of my responsibility, and also a resolute determination that opinions of me held by Buckland and Murchison should not be disappointed. The letter of Dr. Buckland was one of those influences the effect of which was unmitigatedly healthy.

A second edition of this memoir was called for a few years after its first appearance, and to my surprise a third was wanted in 1871.

In my preface to this latter issue, I said : "No
" department of science has made more rapid advances
" than archæology during the last thirty years ; and it
" was obvious to me that the crude production of a
"youth of seventeen, published in 1834, was altogether
" unfit for republication in 1871.   I decided therefore
" to rewrite the greater portion of the memoir, and
" thus bring it into harmony with the present state of
" our knowledge on the subject to which it refers."

In the summer of 1835 an apparently trivial but
really important circumstance occurred ; I received
a message from my father, informing me there were
two gentlemen at the museum who wished to see
me.   I went, and found there Mr. Ransome, surgeon
of the Manchester Infirmary, and Mr. Binion, his
brother-in-law, then one of the partners in the old
established firm of calico printers in Manchester,
known as John Hoyle & Sons.

Both these gentlemen were members of the Society
of Friends.   I showed them some features of
geological interest in the rocks constituting the
picturesque Castle Hill of Scarborough.

They afterwards invited me to sup with them at
their hotel, in order, as they expressed it, to have
a little interchange of ideas.   During the evening
this interchange was commenced by Mr. Ransome
saying rather abruptly :   " William Williamson, thou
" must not remain at Scarborough ; it is no place for
"thee to spend thy life in."   Startled by the suggestion,
I could only point out, that I saw no other course

open to me. After a few additional remarks of the same kind, the subject was dropped. At that time there resided in Scarborough an independent gentleman, Mr. John Bury, who had originally been a merchant in Manchester. Having now no special occupation, he took considerable interest in the museum, and though making no pretence whatever at being a scientific man, he was ever ready to accompany us on our scientific excursions.

A few weeks after the Ransome episode he one day called at the surgery to tell me that an influential physician from Manchester was about to spend a few days at his house, and that he wished me to join their dinner circle on the following day. On arriving at Mr. Bury's house, I found Dr. Chas. Phillips, one of the physicians to the Manchester Infirmary, who also took considerable interest in geological and biological subjects. In order to obtain some knowledge of the geology of the Yorkshire coast, we arranged an excursion for the following day among the Liassic rocks of the Peak Hill and Robin Hood's Bay. During that day, the inadequacy of Scarborough to supply me with a future career was again urged by Dr. Phillips. There had evidently been some communication between him and my former visitors from Manchester; but, so far as I was concerned, my views underwent no change. I told him that two years remained before my apprenticeship to Mr. Weddell would expire, and I must complete my medical education, in order to live. He then told me they wanted a

curator for a season at the museum of the Manchester
Natural History Society, and, that if I would go, it
need make no serious break in my preparations for
a medical career, because Mr. Ransome, my previous
visitor, was prepared to have my indenture transferred from Mr. Weddell to himself, without any fee,
by which arrangement great medical privileges would
be available to me in Manchester.   But all was in
vain.   I was so stupidly wedded to the idea that it
was my fate to remain in Scarborough that I declined
even to entertain the proposition.   Thus the movement Manchesterwards apparently again terminated.
But now came one of those trivial so called accidents,
far from uncommon in life, and that are so often
turning points.   A day or two later I was carrying
a bottle of medicine to a patient who resided outside " The Bar."   On approaching this venerable
structure, I saw the York mail standing at the door
of Millar's Inn, to pick up a passenger.

Hearing some one call my name, I looked up and
discovered Dr. Phillips on the top of the coach.
He inquired whether my views had undergone
any change ; but before I had time to answer his
query, the coach started.   Shouting hastily back,
he asked, " May I write to you ? "   Seeing no reason
why he should not do that, I simply nodded assent,
and in another moment the coach was alike out of
sight and out of hearing.

This little incident, so accidentally brought about,
was scarcely remembered by me, until one day my

father brought me a letter, just arrived from Dr. Phillips, which reopened in a definite way the subject of my removal. Thus the mere chance of my passing a certain point where a coach was standing but for a couple of minutes determined my future career. The letter in question invited me to meet the Council of the Manchester Natural History Society on an appointed day, for the consideration of my election to the curatorship of their museum. This summons brought matters to a decision. The invitation, coming in so definite a shape, was duly considered in a friendly council with Mr. Weddell, who, unwilling to let his own interests interfere with mine, offered to resign my indentures of apprenticeship. So, on the day fixed, I found myself face to face with the Manchester council, by whom I was at once appointed to the curatorship, and entered upon the duties of my office towards the close of September 1835.

It may not be undesirable at this point to sketch rapidly the scientific researches that were in progress in North-Eastern Britain during the earlier part of the present century. As may naturally be expected, the young science of Geology came prominently to the front, for two reasons.

This was the field hitherto comparatively neglected, but which now held out the greatest promise of reward to its investigators. The labours of Smith had furnished students of the science with definite standards, especially based on observations made in

the south and south-west of England, as to the
succession of strata occurring on the island. Hence
these two districts, the south-west and north-east,
needed only competent observers to determine what
position the rocks by which he was surrounded
held in the vertical section published by the great
teacher.

A second stimulus to active research was furnished by the physical conditions of the long coast
line, extending from the Humber to the Scottish
border. Smith had called attention to the fact that
the " Eastern side of the Island is, therefore, best
"for the commencement of regular observations on
" the organised fossils which are illustrative of its
" geology" ("Strata Identified," p. 2). The uppermost
of the series of the regularly stratified rocks was the
chalk. That fossiliferous beds existed above, and of
more recent origin than this cretaceous stratum
was expected; but years were to pass before
any attempt was made to classify and determine
their exact order and superposition. Hence, as
I have just observed, the series, the succession
of which had been practically determined by Smith,
began with the chalk of Flamborough Head,
the inland outcrop of which was readily traced
along the sweeping undulations of the Yorkshire
wolds, forming the western boundary of the Vale
of York. In Filey Bay there crops out from
under the chalk a vast mass of blue clay, the
common representative of a series of strata much

more distinctly separated, and consequently classified in the South of England than on this coast.

It was only in 1868 that the genius, energy, and accurate knowledge of my friend Professor Judd, of the southern representatives of the Speeton clays, enabled him to divide them into the several zones which correspond with the several Neocomian strata of the south, resting upon representatives of the Kimmeridge clay and even of the Portland beds. These two latter bring us to the Oolitic series of rocks, which commence more conspicuously at Filey Brig, and extend northwards, in an almost unbroken series, as far as the lofty crags of Rocliffe, where they rest upon the magnificent Liassic series, commencing at the Peak Hill, at the southern end of Robin Hood's Bay, and only terminating northwards at Saltburn.

A more attractive field of research for the young geologist of the period than that which I have traced could not be found in any part of England.

Nearly all the strata thus briefly referred to abounded in fossil remains. It is otherwise now. Inland, each stratum is doubtless as richly supplied as in the past : with this difference, that they are, as a rule, accessible only in quarries and railroad cuttings, whereas the precipices and slopes of the long coast line made them more or less accessible at every point. But further, ages had rolled by, during which no attention whatever was paid to these objects. Hence, even the shore gravels were full of them. In my youthful days, in a casual walk from the stream flowing under the cliff-bridge to the Spa, a space not exceeding a quarter of a mile, I could have collected half a dozen of the ammonites of Whitby and Staithes, brought southwards by the forces that accumulated the clays and gravels of the Drift.

I well remember one occasion when my father and I, walking between Sands End and Kettleness, came to a broad, flat scar, left bare by the retiring tide, rich in fossils. Many of these fossils of the Upper Lias, of which division the scar consisted, were contained in hard spherical concretions, and on approaching the Kettleness Alum Works, we found the scar studded with round balls, which were half embedded in blue shale. A large number of these balls contained the well-known ammonites of the Liassic beds, but from others there projected the solid pointed end of a belemnite, known as the guard or rostrum, whilst, on splitting open the attached spherical concretion, we found in it the broad chambered part of the object known as the phragmacone. In the course of little more than an hour, we filled our two baskets, as well as converted our handkerchiefs into bags, and before we reached the summit of the Kettleness cliff, on our way to our resting-place for the night, we found that our burdens were quite as much as our strength enabled us to carry. I refer to this expedition to illustrate the abundance with which fossils could be

obtained in those days on various parts of the Yorkshire coast. In more recent times I have travelled
over the same ground without discovering a single
fossil worth carrying away. On one late occasion,
when twitting one of my Scarborough friends with
the absence of the geological energies displayed by
the townsmen of my earlier days, he retorted very
truthfully, " It is all very well for you fellows to
" reprove us in that way, seeing that you cleared
" the coast so completely that you left us nothing
" to do."

Besides my father and Mr. Bean, we had at
Scarborough in those days a class of working men
who devoted most of their time to collecting these
fossils for sale. One called Rudd or Reed, and
another whom we always recognised by the name of
Irish Peter, were long known as the most skilful of
their class, and who also well knew the worth of a
new fossil when they found one. It was mainly by
the labours of these two men that Mr. Leckenby
brought together the fine collection of Oolitic
fossils afterwards purchased by Sedgwick, and now
in the Cambridge Museum. There were at the
same time a few similar men in the coast towns of
Bridlington, Filey, and Whitby. But at the latter
place Messrs. Young and Bird, the former geologist
the latter artist, were also accumulating the collection
now preserved in the Whitby Museum, and writing
the work which in 1822 they published conjointly,
under the name of "A Geological Survey of the

"Yorkshire Coast." The competence of Young to write such a book may be judged by the following quotation from it :

"Instead of assigning such high antiquity to the "whole of the strata, why may we not rather "suppose that a great proportion of them, particu-"larly such as contain organic remains, might be "formed at the era of the Deluge ? We are far "from adopting on this subject the crude opinions "of Dr. Woodward ; yet we are persuaded that he "and Mr. Howard and others who ascribe to the "Deluge the principal changes which the crust of "our globe has undergone, in so far come nearer "the truth than those who would throw back those "changes into long ages that preceded the creation "of man, involving them in the darkness of the "chaos." This quotation is a fair example of the prejudiced rubbish with which the true men of science had to contend. At the same time, Bird, a most amiable artist, prepared some coarse but other-wise recognisable figures of many of the more common of the East Yorkshire fossils, and the diagrams of the strata from Spurn Head to Hartle-pool gave a fair outline of the coast, with its rocky foreshore and its "Hinter" land of Yorkshire hills. Contemporaneously with Young and Bird, John Phillips, a youth of very different calibre, the nephew and constant companion of William Smith, was laying the foundations of a most profound know-ledge of the same subject. At this time there

existed in York a strong body of scientific men :
The Reverend William Venables Vernon, afterwards
Vernon Harcourt ; Thomas Allis, the ornithologist ;
the three Backhouses, botanists and horticulturists ;
Drs. Beckwith and Belcombe, Mr. James Cooke,
Dr. G. Goldie, Jonathan Gray, and Daniel Tuke, all
interested according to their several tastes in
scientific work.   Fortunately, alike for themselves
and for John Phillips, they appointed him keeper of
the Museum of the Yorkshire Philosophical Society.
At or very nearly the same time, John Edward Lee
and William Hey Dykes of Hull, E. G. George of
Leeds, and Mr. Ripley of Whitby were prosecuting
similar scientific studies.   Thus, these towns became
centres from which a scientific impetus diffused
itself throughout Eastern Yorkshire.

I have already referred to the publication by John
Phillips of the first part of his " Illustrations of the
" Geology of Yorkshire," and its effects upon my own
taste and life.   Under such a combination of
influences, no wonder that in crossing the county
border, we find at Newcastle another cluster of
eminent workers.   The centre of an important coal
district was sure to be supplied with eminent
colliery engineers, and we found them in such men
as Buddle and Sopworth.   William Hutton, one of
the authors of the " Fossil Flora of Great Britain,"
was the local authority on fossil plants.   William
Hewitson was then publishing his beautiful work on
" Eggs of the British Birds," as well as laying the

foundations for his superb collection of British and foreign butterflies; Joshua Alder and Albany Hancock were writing their "Investigations of the "Nudibranchiate Molluscs"; John Hancock was steadily rising to be a high authority on British birds, and to be one of the most accomplished taxidermists that Great Britain has ever known; and William Bowman was the local representative of the English botanists: a galaxy of distinguished men rarely equalled in any provincial town. At the same time we had at Durham Professor Johnson, the leader in all questions of Agricultural Chemistry, and but a little further north, Berwick was the home of Johnstone, the author of the "History of British "Zoophytes."

CHAPTER IV

IF, before my acceptance of the curatorship of
the Manchester Museum I had known all I subsequently learned, I should certainly have shrunk
from taking the step. The museum of the Natural
History Society, with which I now became con-

nected, had been in existence many years, under
the care of an uneducated [man named Harrop
—a man wholly ignorant of every branch of
science except taxidermy, and he was probably
the most accomplished bird-stuffer in Europe.
Singularly enough, when my father was curator
of the Scarborough Museum, its council, knowing
that the formation of a collection of British birds
would be an important part of his duties, sent
him to Manchester to learn the art of bird-stuffing
from this very man. Harrop proved an admirable
teacher, and I in turn benefited by learning the same
art from his pupil.

Harrop naturally resented so young a man being
placed over his head in the Society where he had
reigned supreme. The greater and unscientific part
of the council were in friendly sympathy with their
old servant, but a few men of different stamp had
recently been placed upon that council. These determined that what was then only a collection of orna-
mentally grouped birds should be made into a
scientific museum, not only in the bird, but in all
other departments.

The leader of this reforming party was the Dr.
Phillips whose persevering energy had achieved my
election to the curatorship. He was supported by
Edward Tootal, a leading merchant in Manchester,
not a scientific man, but a reformer of shams and
abuses in every department of life. Further support
of the same kind was given by Dr. James Bardsley,

then undisputed head of the medical profession in the town. Thus, the council was composed of two parties—the one of progress, the other of " *laisser faire.*" One battle had been fought over the letter of invitation sent to me, another on the question of my salary. It was originally proposed that this should be the same as was given to the taxidermist; but Dr. Bardsley shrewdly saw that my supremacy as curator could not be maintained along with identity of salary. Hence he proposed and carried a notion that mine should be raised to £110 per annum—£10 in excess of Harrop's—much to the disgust of the friends of the latter on the council.

Thus thrown into a Society composed of two hostile camps, and being the elected administrative instrument of only one of them, my position was very uncomfortable. Moreover, my difficulties for some time increased rather than diminished. Almost immediately after my appointment Dr. William Henry, the then distinguished chemist, proposed to the Literary and Philosophical Society of Manchester that I should be invited to attend its meetings, as if I were a regular member, making at the same time some flattering remarks, very encouraging to the poor, half-bewildered youth. At that time the geology of the districts immediately around Manchester was very imperfectly understood. A succession of layers of limestone cropped out in the bed of the river Medlock on the north-east side of the town. In the elevated ground overhanging

the north bank of the stream, these limestones had
been excavated by means of subterranean workings
for a great number of years. Geologically they were
known by the name of Ardwick limestones. The
question of the age and geological position of these
strata had never been satisfactorily determined, but
Dr. William Henry was supposed to have settled
the points when he announced that the rock contained some seven per cent. of magnesia. This determination, coming from a chemist of high reputation,
and who was also the inventor of the then celebrated preparation of calcined magnesia, was regarded
as a proof that the Ardwick limestones were the
equivalents of the magnesian limestones of Durham.

A short time previously the late Mr. Binney and
Mr. John Leigh, subsequently officer of health to the
Manchester Corporation, had discovered some thin
fossiliferous red shales and limestones in the sides
of a drain near the banks of the river Irk, at Collyhurst. It so happened that their paper announcing
this discovery was read at the first meeting of the
Literary and Philosophical Society that I was able
to attend. The two authors were in doubt respecting the stratum indicated by these fossils. But I,
on examining the specimens on the table with which
they illustrated their paper, recognised their identity
with some of the most characteristic fossils of the true
Durham magnesian limestone. The most important
of these fossils was " Aximus obscurus," subsequently known as " Schizodus obscurus."

Since both the beds and the fossils which they contained were clearly different from anything seen in the Ardwick limestones, it was obvious that Dr. Henry's suggestions as to the age and geological position of these latter strata were mistaken ones. It soon became evident that the Ardwick limestones belonged to the uppermost portions of the carboniferous series.

In October 1836, I communicated to Vol. IX. of the third series of the *London and Edinburgh Philosophical Magazine* a memoir on the " Limestones " Found in the Vicinity of Manchester," giving a full account of their relative positions and of the fossils which they contained, so far as the latter objects were then known to us.

Encouraged by the results of the meeting just recorded, Dr. Phillips took another step. He informed me that a part of my duty to the Society whose officer I had just become, consisted in working out the general geology of the district, and seeing that I had been correct in my identification of the Collyhurst beds, and having heard that similar beds were exposed in a cutting of the line of the recently constructed Manchester and Liverpool Railway, he sent me off to examine and report upon them. I obeyed his instructions, but when, after my return, he laid before the treasurer my little bill of expenses the storm broke out anew. The then treasurer was Mr. Thomas Fleming, a remarkable but aged man, who had made a large fortune in one of those by-

ways possible only in the midst of a large community.

Mr. Fleming was one of the most determined
opponents of the reforming party; hence my bill
acted like the traditional red rag to a bull. In the
heated discussion which ensued, one of the opposition accused Dr. Phillips of uttering an untruth. At
that time one of the members of council was a
surgeon of the name of Mann, who had spent the
earlier part of his life in the army. The moment
the stormy council meeting broke up, Dr. Phillips
went direct to Mr. Mann's house, and asked him, as
one familiar with the usages of the army, what course
he ought to adopt after the public insult he had
just received. At that time the duello, though on
the wane, had not yet been permanently banished
from English society. So Mr. Mann replied that
there was but one course open to him. Phillips then
asked his friend to be the bearer of a hostile message
to the offending individual. An old army man could
scarcely decline such a mission, and Mr. Mann at once
departed on his errand. It was arranged that Dr.
Phillips should await his friend's return at Mr.
Mann's own house.

The most solemn affairs have occasionally their
ludicrous aspects, and such were not wanting
here. Looking out of the window of the room
in which he was waiting, into Deansgate, Dr.
Phillips saw two policemen walking backwards
and forwards in front of the house, and at once

jumped to the conclusion that they were watching him. The idea that Mr. Mann had betrayed him gained strength by the fact, that the messenger was much longer absent than appeared to be necessary. So poor Phillips, who was by nature proud and irascible, gradually worked himself into a white heat of passion, and when Mr. Mann at last returned he was somewhat astonished at the outburst of temper with which he was received. In his excitement Dr. Phillips had forgotten that Mr. Mann's house was next door to the Deansgate Police Station, and allowed the presence of the policemen off duty to distress him. Mr. Mann had failed to deliver the message with which he was charged, because of his inability to find the individual to whom it was addressed; the challenge reached him, however, ultimately through another channel.

Before answering his challenge, the recipient prudently sought to obtain from a neighbouring magistrate *permission to fight the duel.* This official at once informed him that if the quarrel went one step further, he should instantly arrest both him and his challenger, and so the affair came to an end. This disturbance appears to have cleared the atmosphere, and brought about a better state of things in the council chamber. I worked very hard, and even gained the consent of the council to leave the museum at noon on Saturdays, and to remain away until one o'clock on the succeeding Monday, in order to facilitate my investigations amongst the

geological phenomena of the district. Men previously
hostile now gradually became personal friends, and
work progressed smoothly for some time. My first
business in each department was to separate the
British from the foreign collections. The birds, of
which we had for that period a large number, were
the objects to which I first turned my attention.
They were, when I took charge of the museum,
arranged in ornamental groups, without any consideration for their scientific relationships. The
plan which I adopted with the arboreal birds showed
the student at once which belonged to the same
genera. The glazed cases in which they were
preserved were fitted with artificial branches made
of wire and tow and coated with a wash of coloured
size. If I had a bird which was a genus in itself,
it was supported on a single twig fastened to the
woodwork of the case. If, on the other hand, I
was dealing with a genus that contained two or
more species, a tree was made for them, having as
many twigs as there were birds to be placed upon
them ; so the boundaries of each genus were seen at
a glance.

As I have already indicated, there were amongst
us two or three men whose science was of the
shallowest type, and upon whom the wags of the
town sometimes played sad tricks. On one occasion
a pseudo-ornithologist was thus " taken in." The
humourist, who had extensive gardens around his
house, called upon our amateur friend and announced

that a new bird had been seen in his grounds with a remarkable red neck.

The ornithologist at once accepted the invitation to visit his friend's place and see the bird for himself, which he did clearly enough, and immediately called for a gun and shot a poor little robin, which had been accidentally caught in a trap, and had had a bit of red rag stitched round his neck, in order to hoax our ambitious would-be discoverer. On another occasion one of the same fraternity, but who claimed to be an authority on angling, was cheated in a similar way. He was informed that a notable discovery had been made in a neighbouring sheet of fresh water, viz., that salt water herrings had been found in it living, and he was invited to prove the statement for himself. He went, but being very short-sighted, one of the conspirators had no difficulty in fastening a fresh herring to his hook, this the angler landed in some excitement. Not content, however, with having hoaxed our piscatorial friend so far, a second fish was landed in like manner. On looking at it a moment, the angler exclaimed, with a twinkling eye, " Nay, not red ones ! "

Whilst work at the museum progressed, other labours were not neglected. The recent discoveries at Burdie House, near Edinburgh, chronicled by Dr. Hibbert, had attracted much attention, revealing as they did the existence in the carboniferous rocks of a magnificent group of fossil Sauroid fishes. Soon afterwards the Leeds geologists enriched their museum with the superb specimen of the Megalicthys Hibbertii, still one of the gems of their collection. Our endeavours to discover similar objects in the coalfields of Lancashire were soon rewarded. In Volume IX. of the *Philosophical Magazine of London and Edinburgh*, the results of our labours are recorded in my paper already referred to. This paper was followed by an elaborate communication to the British Association at their Liverpool meeting, 1837, on the Coalfields of Western Lancashire, illustrated by a large vertical section of the strata between the uppermost of the Ardwick limestones and the millstone grit. That section is now preserved in the library of the Geological Society of Manchester.

Before closing these records of my earlier years in Manchester, if the picture is to be true, a few words must be added of my more private life. My parents had no special religious views, and when I came to Manchester I shared their indifference on these subjects. For some months after my arrival I was fearfully lonely. Coming as I did from a happy and sympathetic home, and flung suddenly into the midst of a vast population, in which I had neither friend nor acquaintance, I yearned for some society, but none offered itself to me. Dr. Phillips, who brought me to the town, had one of those stern natures to whom the emotional and sympathetic sides of boyhood were unknown. Though meeting him almost daily at the museum, it did not appear to occur to him that a youth should wish some form of life outside that museum. I was never once invited into his house, and never entered it except when museum matters required me to do so. My lodgings were comfortless, and my evenings solitary and wretched. Whilst suffering this depressing, miserable loneliness, I one day met accidentally in the street a lad of my own age, whom I had known in Scarborough. At that time, a highly respectable and clever family of the name of Beverley were lessees of the theatre of my native town, and were old acquaintances. One of the sons of this family was William Beverley, the celebrated artist and scene-painter. My young friend was nephew of William Beverley, and grandson of the lessee. He told me his father had become manager of the Queen's Theatre in Manchester, and my name was at once put upon the " free list." Having been trained at home to enjoy theatrical performances, I revelled in this release from my weary solitude, and spent night after night in the boxes of the Queen's Theatre, with, of course, easy access to the Green Room. The dangers of such a position to a pure but inexperienced lad were inevitable, and must have resulted in wrong, but for help of another and far better kind.

One afternoon a merchant of the name of Yates called upon me at the museum, to invite me to accompany him to his house. I found that a brother-in-law of this gentleman was visiting Scarborough, and had there heard of my appointment in Man-

chester ; and, deeming I should probably be devoid
of social comforts, he had asked Mr. Yates to look
after me. I found my new friend a kind and
benevolent member of the Wesleyan Methodist
Society, and an earnest reader of scientific books,
though not a practical man of science. Mr. Yates'
house became from time to time a veritable haven of
rest to me, especially in seasons of temporary in-
disposition. In a few weeks Mr. T. R. Williams,
the brother-in-law, had returned from Scarborough,
and his home in like manner was opened to me.
Through these friends I was introduced to a third
Wesleyan, Mr. W. H. Johnstone, a partner in the
great house of A. and S. Henry & Co., and who also
treated me with a kindness never to be forgotten.

The benefit which these three families conferred
by their unselfish thoughtfulness towards the lonely
and almost friendless student taught me a lesson,
upon which I have endeavoured to act during my
own maturer life, viz., the beneficent influence that
a little kind attention to lonesome lads may produce,
in thus bringing them under the influences of happy
homes.

One result of these friendly acts was to familiarise
me with Wesleyan circles, and led to my being a
member of that religious body for some years. My
geology prevented me from ever accepting many of
the doctrines propounded from their pulpits, but I
can never express too strongly or too kindly the
good influence which this union with Methodism

exercised over me. It shielded me from perils that thickly strewed my path, until I attained to years and a social position, in which I was safe against the temptations that bring so many youths to ruin. I may also mention here that the introduction to these three families led at a later period to one of the most important events of my life. It was at the house of Mr. Johnstone I met with the lady who, in 1842, became my wife, and with whom I lived in happy union for a period of twenty-nine years.

In the summer of 1838 the time appeared to me to have arrived for resigning my curatorship and preparing to resume my medical studies. The former I did in June, intending to become student in one of the two competing medical schools of Manchester, when its next session should commence in October. But the important fact stared me in the face, that funds were required for carrying out this plan. I had already provided diagrams and a small collection of fossils, in illustration of a course of six public lectures on geology, and I then made arrangements for their delivery in various towns where I happened to have personal friends. I began my series at Bolton, in Lancashire, and continued it in Wigan, Warrington, Blackburn, Knaresborough, Harrogate, Ripon, Scarborough, and Hull. The work was hard, and its remuneration limited; nevertheless, the money thus earned served to carry me through the winter session, including the payment of medical school fees; and to supply me with pocket-money for the subsequent summer. In those days, student life in Manchester schools was somewhat Bohemian. Though there were one or two lecturers of the professional calibre of the late Sir James Bardsley and Mr. Jordan, most of them were decidedly men of but ordinary powers; amongst these were several who were not only commonplace teachers but irregular in attendance. The dissecting-room was left entirely in the hands of students, no official superintending teacher having been appointed. A not uncommon occupation of the students was to gather in a semicircle round the fire, and exercise their talent of glee singing; that is, when they were not actually engaged in more mischievous schemes. The "subjects," by the dissection of which, in those days, medical students acquired their knowledge of human anatomy, were obtained from the prisons and the workhouses, but people who died in the latter abodes were carefully protected by the Anatomy Act. Any relative or friend could claim a dead person, and prevent him or her from being transmitted to a medical school. Not only so, but a dying inmate of a workhouse could authorise the master of the house thus to protect him. With each " subject " arriving at the school, a coffin was sent to receive "the remains " when they had served their purpose; which remains were forwarded for interment to a particular church, in one of the suburbs of Manchester. On one occasion, a lecturer had acquired a dead donkey, which was brought into our dissecting-room to be skeletonised for its owner. When this was accomplished, all other "remains" of the animal were put, by some of the mischief-loving students, into one of the vacant coffins, and the coffin sent as usual to church for interment; the mischievous young monkeys attending in order to witness the clergyman perform the solemn service of burial over his "dear departed brother."

Meanwhile, the really earnest workers had, under such unsatisfactory conditions, no alternative but to make the best use they could of their imperfect helps to study. After a weary and very depressing winter the session came to a close, and I left the town for three months' fresh air in my native Scarborough, previous to continuing my medical education in London.

Before, however, leaving the Manchester of this period, I should like to give an idea, necessarily a slight one, of the scientific men by whom I was surrounded.

Of course our most distinguished "man of science" was the then veteran John Dalton. He was rarely absent from his seat in a warm corner of the room during the meetings of the Literary and Philosophical Society. Though a sober-minded Quaker, he was not devoid of some sense of fun; and there was a tradition amongst us, not only that he had once been a poet, but that, although a bachelor, two manuscript copies were still extant of his verses on the subject of matrimonial felicity; and it is my belief there was foundation for the tradition. The old man was sensitive on the subject of his age. Dining one day at the hospitable board of Dr. Edward Holmes, he was placed between two ladies, Mrs. William Henry and her sister, Miss Allen, both daughters of Allen, the distinguished mineralogist, of Edinburgh. These ladies resolved to extract from him some admission on the tender point, but in vain. Though never other than courteous, Dalton foiled all their feminine arts and retained his secret.

During his last illness, when he had only a house-keeper to take care of him, several of us young men undertook to watch in turn by his bedside through the night. On the last occasion when it was my duty to do this, I noticed he looked very pale and restless. Knowing the end could not be far off, I became alarmed, and hastily mixed some hot brandy and water, which he drank quickly. My anxiety was allayed when I heard a fairly audible voice exclaim, " That's good stuff."

Dalton's quaint and diminutive figure was a strongly individualised one. Many portraits of him have been published, but in my opinion none are so graphic as one taken by the late Mr. Stephenson, the well-known engraver, who some years ago sent me a copy of this portrait, along with an account of the circumstances under which it was taken. Mr. Stephenson says :

" Prior to the meeting of the British Association
" in Manchester, it was mooted to me that a good
" characteristic portrait of Dalton would be accept-
" able ; but Peter Clare said the Doctor would not
" sit for a photograph ; so he arranged that I should
" attend a meeting of the Philosophical Society on a
" certain night. I did so, and he (Peter) strongly
" impressed upon me the following words :

" ' Thou must not *make* a sketch, nor be seen
" ' doing anything of that kind, on no account what-
" ' ever. Thou must be seated where I will direct
" ' thee, that thou may be able to look at him.'

" At the appointed time ' Peter' took me to an
" elevated seat at the extreme corner of the lecture
" room, about three or four yards from where the
" Doctor sat. A member introduced a small article,
" and read a paper, followed by a discussion ; then
" the Doctor rose and, taking the instrument, held it
" up to examine it. Now, that was the important
" moment for me to be impressed with Dalton's
" attitude. I assure you it was the most anxious
" and trying time in my experience, lest my memory
" should fail before I got home. When the meeting
" was over, I spoke to no one, saw Peter escort the
" Doctor across the street, a dark, dirty, damp night.
" I hastened to the Cheetham Hill omnibus and got
" home, not allowing a word or object to divert my
" mind from what I had seen. After refreshment, I
" got out a sheet of Bristol board, and sketched, very
" roughly and faintly, with a lead pencil, the head of

" Dalton in the position I saw it. . . . . My intention,
" when I first made the original sketch, was to bring
" out a highly-finished engraving . . . . but P. C.
" bestirred himself, and persuaded the Doctor to sit
" for a photograph."

After the death of Dalton, we apparently entered
upon a scientific interregnum. There were still men
who in their youth had done good work, but who
were now rapidly passing into the sere and yellow
leaf, and their labours were things of the past;
others, whose names we shall meet later, were
young and unformed; and, for the moment, science
of the highest order was not so conspicuous in
Manchester as it became later—trade and politics
chiefly absorbed the intellectual energies of the town.
Still we retained, even during this period of comparative repose, a very distinct social and scientific
circle.

Among the chemists whom Dalton left, William
Henry was certainly the most prominent; perhaps
deservedly so, though he owed his position in the
first instance to his father, Thomas Henry. He was,
later in life, elected Fellow of the Royal Society, and
the subsequent year was awarded the Copley medal.
But he became wealthy, and shared the fate so
common to men to whom that happens: social position and past successes combined to establish a reputation; and, apparently content with this, he made
no effort to keep pace with the advances chemistry
was rapidly making amongst his young confederates

in France and Germany. At an early meeting of
the British Association, one of these progressive
foreigners treated poor Henry during a chemical
discussion with a contemptuous disrespect that
wounded him deeply; an affront he probably never
afterwards forgot.

Among engineers, the great firm of Sharp,
Roberts & Co. was still in active operation, though
Roberts himself, the inventive partner, was no longer
what he had been when his new machinery was so
materially influencing the cotton-spinning processes.
Sir William Fairbairn was not yet culminated,
though he and his mathematical co-worker, the late
Eaton Hodgkinson, laid from time to time, before
our Society, observations on the strength of various
materials that have wonderfully facilitated modern
constructive operations. Less frequently Whitworth
was present; he was then perfecting machines capable of measuring a bar to the minutest fraction of
an inch, and already making those self-acting tools
and standards of measurement that are now in use
in every part of the world.

In the various branches of natural science, however, Manchester even at this period had its devotees.
One Mr. Blackwall, an entomologist, came to the
front, and was our highest authority respecting the
species and classification of spiders. Mr. James
Aspinall Turner, at one time Parliamentary member
for Manchester, was accumulating a fine collection of
foreign Coleoptera.

In geology, Mr. Binney, a young solicitor, began
to pay some attention to coal and collieries; not
because he cared for such subjects, but avowedly
because he thought that, in becoming an authority
on them, he might obtain the confidence of great
colliery proprietors, and convert them into clients.
In this respect I fear he was not successful, but he
certainly became one of the chief geologists of the
district. Some time previously, a young letter-
press printer named Looney had been making good
geological observations, but other duties called
him away, and fossil-hunting fell into the back-
ground.

The botanical interests of the district were chiefly
in the hands of the operative community. The hills
between Lancashire and Yorkshire swarmed with
botanical and floricultural societies, who met on
Sundays, the only day on which it was possible to
do so. Our highest authority on the native plants
was a poor old working-man named Buxton; the
little work which he published under the name of
" A Botanical Guide to the Flowering Plants, Ferns,
" Mosses, and Algæ found indigenous within sixteen
" miles of Manchester, with some Information as to
" their Agricultural, Medicinal, and other Uses," has
not yet been surpassed. Richard Buxton was
entirely self-educated, and in a brief preface to his
little guide, he gives an interesting sketch of his history
and companions. We here find notice of such men as
Horsefield, Percival, Crowther, Crozer, and Tinker,

whose names are well known to me as leaders in these botanical circles, and with some of whom I was personally well acquainted. They and their hundreds of companions constituted the true workers in the botanical field of Lancashire. To show the spirit which pervaded them I will quote a few lines from Buxton's introduction relative to the societies to which I have referred above. Buxton says, "As specific discrimination and accuracy " in botanical nomenclature are the chief objects " sought to be obtained by the aid of these meet- " ings ; all persons who attend are hereby re- " spectfully solicited to bring with them such speci- " mens of plants, either indigenous or exotic, but " particularly the former, as they can conveniently " procure." The above quotation is an extract from a printed list circulated among the members. But Buxton goes on to say, "The specimens are sub- " mitted to the President, who describes them, and " then discussions upon them take place. The num- " ber of meetings held generally amounted to about " thirty in the course of the year, and the audience " consists almost entirely of working men. No one " knows anything of the origin of this Society, but " its meetings must have been held for near a " century back."

The above was written in 1849, and I believe the same Society is still in existence, if not, there are many others like it.

An incident in the life of Sir Edward Smith illustrates the class of men of whom I have been writing. It was Sir Edward's intention, as soon as the fourth volume of his " English Flora " was off his hands, to prepare a fifth, in order to embrace the cryptogams, and he was desirous of obtaining a better knowledge of the British mosses. At that time there lived in Manchester a man of the name of Edward Hobson, who held a subordinate position in a tea-merchant's shop in Deansgate. This man was an excellent muscologist and had issued a book containing specimens of the plants themselves instead of figures of them. Hobson was a leader amongst the societies noticed above. In that ante-railroad period many passengers travelled to Manchester by canal, the boat terminus of which was at the bridge near the Salford Railway Station. On arriving at this landing-place, Sir Edward having obtained a porter of the unofficial type that so commonly hang about termini, to carry his portmanteau to one of the hotels of the town, inquired on the way of his attendant, " Do you happen to know a man of the name of " Edward Hobson ? " " Dun ya mean Hobson the " botanist ? " Smith answered in the affirmative, and the man replied, " Yea, I do." Smith, rather wondering at this, inquired how he had got to know him, when his companion intimated that he and Hobson often went out together collecting mosses. Smith next asked, " Do you know anything about " mosses ? " which question again elicited an affirmative response. The confabulation ended in Smith's engaging this man to be, for some weeks, his guide through the district, and the man was able to show Sir Edward where all the more important mosses were to be seen growing.

In quite a different social atmosphere, but still during the period of which I am now speaking, viz., during the "forties," one Mr. John Moore was favourably known in Manchester circles, especially as a representative of agriculture. He took also a very active part in the management of the Philosophical Society, but he was far from being an intellectually strong man.

Although Mr. Leo Grindon only arrived in Manchester about this time, he began and has continued until now to devote much time to the conduct of botanical societies. He has also written a long series of works on botanical subjects.

Speaking rather socially than scientifically, perhaps the most conspicuous object of our literary and philosophical gatherings was Peter Clare, one of the secretaries of the Society. He was a genial and somewhat fussy little Quaker, the constant friend and ultimately the executor of Dalton. In a brief notice of his life, read before the Society in 1852, its author correctly said, " Mr. Clare was not a pro-"found student, nor was he a frequent contributor "to the publications of any of the literary or "scientific institutions with which he stood con-"nected," yet he was an active man and useful to those institutions.

But one more member of our Society must not be passed over without notice, because though not in any sense a practical man of science, he was a great social power among those who were.

Dr. Edward Holmes was a bachelor physician, who long resided at the upper end of King Street, in a house adjoining Brook's Bank. He was for many years the President of the Literary and Philosophical Society, and an excellent portrait of him hangs in the rooms where our meetings were held. Dr. Holmes was a walking encyclopædia of the literature of Natural History. His habit was to sit reading far into the night with a jug of beer by his side, and, endowed as he was with a marvellous memory, he deservedly obtained a reputation for being the most learned man in the town so far as scientific literature was concerned. Being alike wealthy and hospitable, some of the pleasantest assemblies of the more intelligent inhabitants as well as visitors were to be met with round his social table. I have vivid remembrance of Mrs. Lee, the widow of Major Bowditch, the well-known South African explorer, who on one of these occasions recounted to me an adventure which it was her fate to endure in her first married life. She was in Africa with her husband, the Major, when her health failed, and it was found desirable to send her to England; her husband meanwhile continuing his explorations on the Dark Continent. She sailed and reached her destination, but after a while, becoming weary, she

resolved upon rejoining the Major. Unfortunately
the latter was also becoming lonely, and he resolved
to follow his wife to England. They both sailed
about the same time, and the vessels that were
conveying them in opposite directions met in mid
ocean, exchanged postal packages, and went on
their several ways. Unfortunately the parties so
interested in catching sight of each other failed to do
so, and it was only when they landed, one in England and the other in Africa, that they discovered
what had happened.

The ordinary meetings of our Philosophical Society
were much more social in those days than they have
been in later years. The two principal causes of
this change are not difficult to find. The building
still occupied by the Society was then surrounded on
all sides by private dwellings. No warehouses
existed in any of the neighbouring streets. The
great business centre in those days was Cannon
Street. I well remember when the distinguished
free-trader, Richard Cobden, converted his house in
Mosley Street into a warehouse for the sale of
printed calicoes. This was the first house in this
highly respectable street that was so changed. Many
members of the Society resided here, and others
in George Street, Faulkner Street, or elsewhere
within a few minutes' walk of our meeting rooms.
Hence their attendance involved no difficulty, and
since the gatherings always broke up punctually at
ten minutes past nine, it was no uncommon thing,

for quiet little suppers to be extemporised as pleasant sequels to the more official assemblies. These were easily arranged, because the host frequently resided near the Society's rooms, and his guests were generally not far from their own houses when supper was ended. The huge exodus to villages miles away from the town, now so characteristic of the wealthier part of the Manchester population, had then only begun.

But another change, superadded to that already mentioned, took place; and affected a large portion of the Manchester Society. The dinner-hour was most generally one o'clock; hence the members were not prevented by the intervention of the six or seven o'clock dinner from attending the meetings, as is now the case. Thus, not only were the members attending our meetings reduced, but there was a marked change in the social position of those who did attend.

CHAPTER V

Commencement of medical studentship in London University College—Teaching staff—Fellow students—Search for Fritillaria meleagris—Geological Society—Syrian fossils—Attic lodgings and life—Niger expedition—College caps and gowns—Final examinations—Return to Manchester—Commencement of practice—Operation for strabismus—Mantell's " Medals of Creation "—My father's "Culpepper "—Mr. Joseph Sidebotham—Microscopic observation—Elected member of Manchester Literary and Philosophical Society—Lyon Playfair and Dr. Joule—Sturgeon—Potato disease—Clairvoyance—Braid and hypnotism—False hypnotism.

AFTER leaving Manchester I spent three summer months with my parents, and worked up my Latin in preparation for passing the examination in that language at the Apothecaries' Hall, in the beginning of October; which I succeeded in doing. I was thus enabled to devote myself henceforth to purely medical studies; but financial difficulties still weighed upon my mind. The heavy expenses of college and hospital life, along with those fees which had to be paid at the end of my studentship for admission to the Apothecaries' Hall and the College of

Surgeons, were serious.   However, kind friends lent
me what was necessary; or I must have broken down.
I left Scarborough for London on the last day of
September 1840, and entered myself as student of
University College, nearly emptying my pockets of
its borrowed funds in payment of fees, but my father
was able to send me further help during the winter
term.   I soon found the difference between London
and the provincial schools.   With such men as
Quain in anatomy, Sharpey in physiology, Liston
and Cooper in surgery, C. B. Williams in the chair
of medicine, Graham as professor of chemistry, and
Lindley* of botany, no man with brains could fail
to learn.   Besides these, there were assistant phy-

---

* On entering his name for the class in botany, young
Williamson found one of his teachers would be Professor
Lindley, with whom he had been connected years before in
his drawings and descriptions of plants for " Yorkshire
" Fossil Flora."   He gave his name, " W. C. Williamson."
" W. C. Williamson," repeated Mr. Lindley.   He looked
at the white-faced, delicate lad before him and thought,
" Oh, son or grandson of our correspondent perhaps," but
said, " W. C. Williamson from where ? "   " Scarborough,"
answered the youth; a small, conscious smile tucking
itself away in his sleeve, meanwhile, " Scarborough,"
repeated Professor Lindley.   " Are you then in any way
" related to one, W. C. Williamson, with whom we corre-
" sponded some time ago ? "   " I had the pleasure, sir, of
" corresponding with you myself some years ago."   " You,
" yourself!"   And the teacher in botany began to wonder
whether student or professor would have the better time.—
A. C. W.

sicians and surgeons, who gave high promise of
future eminence. The resident house physician was
Dr. John Taylor, the first man who received Doctor's
Degree from the newly founded University of
London. As a painstaking student and teacher, he
was, in my experience, unrivalled, and had he lived,
nothing could have prevented him from taking the
highest rank amongst Metropolitan physicians. But
unfortunately, the severity with which he pursued
his studies brought on disease of the heart, which
soon drove him into the country. He retreated to
Huddersfield, his native town, where he at once
took the foremost medical position.

Among my fellow-students in the college were
several hard-working men who subsequently attained
high professional rank. Sir William Jenner was
just closing his student's career as I entered upon
mine. Professor Erichsen and Sir Alfred Garrod
rose steadily into the distinguished positions which
they eventually occupied, and which Edmund Parkes
would have attained to, had not an early death
arrested his promising career. My student friend,
Dr. Charles Hare, is my friend still, and to his
kindly care during a nasty illness a year ago I
probably owe my life, now at the age of seventy-
seven.

I availed myself to the uttermost of the brilliant
advantages which such a school afforded me. I was
only once absent from my place in the lecture-room
and hospital, and that was when a brother botanist,

the late Mr. Moore of York, and I determined upon
a pedestrian ramble through the meadows between
Kew and Mortlake in order to see Fritillaria meleagris
growing in its native swamps. At the same time I
occasionally relieved the monotony of study by
spending an evening at a meeting of the Geological
Society, then in the very climax of its youthful and
energetic career. There I had the pleasure of
associating with such men as Sedgwick, Murchison,
Graham, Lonsdale, Greenhow, James Yates, the
Marquis of Northampton, Mantell, Sir Philip Egerton,
Lord Cole, afterwards Earl of Enniskillen, and
Captain Basil Hall—a galaxy of geological stars of
whom not one remains.

I was only once tempted to touch practical
geological work. Professor Graham, afterwards
Master of the Mint, and the author of the scientific
discovery of the functional difference between
colloids and crystalloids, was extremely kind to
me. He had applied to a friend in Syria to send
him some mineral bodies from that region, but when
at length a case arrived, he found it to contain
nothing but fossils; these he handed over to me,
that I might make practical use of them. They
came from Beyrout and the Lebanon district, about
the geology of which very little was known at that
time. I soon found they were of the greatest
interest, having among them fossils of extreme
rarity; hence I drew up a brief memoir descriptive
of them, which I read to the Geological Society.

To the Marquis of Northampton, then the President of the Royal Society, I was indebted, not only for the privilege of attending the meetings of that Society, but also for the pleasure of being present at the magnificent soirées which the President gave from time to time at his noble mansion in Piccadilly.

Through the entire period of my London studentship, I lodged in two minute attics in the house of a tailor in Grafton Street, opposite the eastern end of the College Hospital. My slender finance compelled me to practise the severest economy, my dinner consisting on most days of meat sausages, which I was able to purchase at a few pence per pound. They were fairly good, and I asked no questions as to what they were made of.

I was sustained by a hopeful disposition and a resolute determination to make the best possible use of such opportunities as chance might throw in my way. Nevertheless, I worked daily under the heavy pressure of financial anxieties, which at times, in spite of myself, almost crushed all energy.

I had, before leaving Manchester, become engaged to the lady upon whom my affections had long been centred, and through these months of anxiety and over-work the bright, hopeful letters, which I received from her, acted as an unfailing stimulant and encouragement, saving me, I believe, from despondency, which might have become too great to be endured.

My engagement in all probability also saved me from having my career cut short at an early period.

Soon after the marriage of the Queen to Prince Albert, a movement was set on foot for sending an expedition, with half benevolent, half ulterior commercial purposes, up the River Niger, and a very large meeting of influential persons was held in Exeter Hall to promote this design. The meeting, at which I was present, was presided over by Prince Albert, his first appearance in public after his marriage. The speakers included Sir Robert Peel, the Rev. S. Wilberforce, subsequently Bishop of Oxford and still later of Winchester, and other equally prominent men. A short time after, the close of my winter term at University College having set me free, I had run down to my Scarborough home for a little rest and fresh air before the commencement of the summer medical term. Whilst I was sitting with my father one day, a letter was handed to him by the postman, after reading which, it was passed over to me. It stated a meeting on the subject of the Niger Expedition had been held at the residence of Lord Palmerston, where it was resolved that a naturalist should be appointed to accompany the expedition, and that the post should be offered to me, but that the meeting was not prepared to communicate directly with me until my father had been consulted, in order to learn whether or not such an arrangement would meet with his sanction. Already engaged as

I was to my future wife, and hastening to settle down as medical man in Manchester, happily for me I at once declined the offer.

I say happily, since the expedition was sent forth, and the results were most disastrous. The appointment declined by me was accepted by Dr. Stanger, whose acquaintance I had made some years previously, and whose name is now associated with a remarkable genus of Cycas, viz., Cycad Stangeria, which he discovered in South Africa at a much later date.

The expedition made its way for a considerable distance up the river, but was ultimately brought to a standstill in an atmosphere charged with the most deadly of African miasmata. It became absolutely necessary to get the steamer back to the coast if a single life was to be saved. But there was no one left in a condition to navigate the ship. Crew, captain, and engineer, were alike down with the fearful fever. The only men on board with any pretensions to health and strength were my substitute, Dr. Stanger, who knew nothing of either navigation or steam engines, and a second man who was equally ignorant of these subjects. There was, however, no time for delay. One of these men found a book on steam engines, and undertook the work to be done below, and the other hunted out the river charts, and placed himself at the helm. These two brave men together successfully brought the ship and its remaining invalids down to the pure air of the open sea.

During my first winter in London a movement was started amongst us, not for the first time in the history of the college, advocating the wearing of caps and gowns by the students, and it fell to my lot to open the debate. The officials of the college looked so good-naturedly upon what we were doing as actually to suspend for the day all lectures. I should say the men of St. Bartholomew's and other medical schools looked with great jealousy upon ours in Gower Street, to which, I never knew on what foundation, they gave the name of "Old "Stinkamalee." It so happened that in advocating the change which we contended for, I used the argument that the world was materially influenced by symbols; that men were familiar with caps and gowns at Oxford, Cambridge and other colleges as an indication of studentship, and that, our students having no such visible symbol, we were regarded as a half-and-half sort of a college.

The leader of the opposition was an old student of the college, now practising as dentist with his uncle, at that time the head of this branch of the profession. A day or two after our meeting the following *brochure* from his pen appeared in one of the medical journals :

> " Mr. Williamson thinks he has found out the cause
> Why ' Old Stinkamalee ' gains so little applause :
> Oxonians may smile, St. Bartholomew's laugh,
> University College is but half-and-half."

To a Londoner this *jeu d'esprit* was irresistible.

At last the time drew near for me to enter for my medical examinations at the Apothecaries' Hall and the College of Surgeons, both of which I passed safely. My principal examiner was the late Sir Astley Cooper. It was usual at that time for each student to pass his examination successively in front of four tables, behind each of which two examiners were seated. But on this occasion one of the tables was unoccupied. After Cooper and his colleague had done with me, I looked inquiringly, asking where I was to go next; but was answered by Sir Astley's fellow examiner: "Are you not "satisfied? Have you not had enough?"

"Not he!" said the bright and smiling veteran baronet. "He evidently likes it."

My London work was now finished, and I returned to Manchester, with very vague impressions as to what was next to happen. This question was, however, soon determined for me. Two valued friends —Mr. Bury, of Scarborough, whose name I have already mentioned, and Mr. John Mayson, a well-known Manchester merchant—came to my assistance. The communication from each was virtually the same—viz., "I know that your finances are "exhausted, but start on your medical career, and "draw upon me for any money you may require." I accepted their very generous offer, acted upon their recommendation, and on January 1, 1841, mounted my brass-plate on the door of a house which is now

a tobacconist's shop at the corner of Wilton Street
and Oxford Road.

An old medical friend gave me some excellent
practical advice. He said : " You will have for some
" time to go much oftener down steps than up steps.
" Never mind! win the good opinions of washerwomen
" and such like, and in time you will hear of their
" recommendations of you to the wealthier families by
" whom they are employed." I did so, and found it
succeed as predicted.

The ordinary experiences of the life of most young
medical practitioners need not be recorded, but some
special ones had value in my case. One of the
newest operations in surgery that had attracted
my attention just before I left London, was that
which proved to be a cure for strabismus or squint-
ing. As a practical remedy, the knowledge of this
operation had not reached the provinces. The report
of two or three successful attempts of this kind
performed in Manchester spread abroad, and besides
bringing me a number of patients who were similarly affected, brought to me also a youth (with a fair
fee) whose friends wished me to receive him into my
house as medical pupil. This led a short time afterwards to my obtaining a second resident pupil. I
was, early in my career, appointed medical superintendent to a large club of Oddfellows, and thus, in
various ways, I passed through the first two years
without having to borrow very much from my kind
friends.

Meanwhile, I carefully avoided every identification of myself with the scientific circles of Manchester, knowing well how jealous the public was of all such pursuits until a medical man was thoroughly established; after that he might do as he liked.

In June 1842 I married the lady to whom I had been so long engaged—a step which proved to be the commencement of a happy career. About this time an apparently trifling incident brought about a change to more scientific pursuits. My wife and I one day joined the tea-table of a friend, a Methodist widow lady, who, my wife urged, would be much gratified by our doing so. It is difficult to conceive of any circle less likely to exercise a scientific influence over me than that which we had promised to join. Nevertheless, that was exactly what it did. During the evening a gentlemanly and intelligent young nephew of our hostess joined the gathering, and asked me if I had seen Dr. Mantell's new work, "Medals of Creation." Having to answer in the negative, he kindly offered to lend me his copy, which he did a day or two later.

Perusing the interesting volume, I came upon some passages in which the author gave an abstract of Ehrenberg's now well-known discovery, that native chalk really consisted largely of a mass of microscopic calcareous shells. Startled by this information, I naturally longed to see these objects, but I had no microscope. I remembered, however, that my father at Scarborough had an old "Culpepper," which I asked him to send to me. The wretched old instrument certainly revealed these minute organisms, though very imperfectly. I then sought the aid of Mr. Dancer, the well-known optician of Manchester, in making some changes in the old instrument to give it better defining power. This was accomplished to a limited but unsatisfactory extent.

At that time Dancer was constructing some beautiful, but in my eyes very costly microscopes, apparently out of my reach. Meanwhile I became personally acquainted with Dr. Mantell, and we exchanged letters almost weekly. Stimulated partly by him, and partly by association with Mr. Joseph Sidebotham, then a young merchant, but already an enthusiastic entomologist as well as a practical botanist, studying especially the lower confervæ, Diatomaceæ, and Desmidiacæ, and who became ultimately head of one of the oldest firms of calico-printers in Manchester; I found myself drawn *nolens volens* into the vortex of microscopic observation, which was ultimately so largely the work of my life, an wholly unexpected result of my visit to the aged widow's tea-party. Progress in my professional position encouraged me to be less fearful of the scientific occupation of my leisure hours being known, and I was elected member, and henceforth attended the meetings, of the Manchester Literary and Philosophical Society. At one of these meetings, a young man of the name of Playfair, recently from Germany, made his appearance, and was introduced to me. It was rumoured in the meeting that this youth had in his pocket a translation into English of Liebig's celebrated work on agricultural chemistry, which proved to be true, and the translation was soon afterwards published. Another evening, a young and extremely unassuming man appeared, who was introduced to me as a Mr. Joule. The first of these visitors is now Baron Playfair, the second, the man whose death all philosophers have recently deplored, and whose statue now stands in the Town Hall of Manchester. Another remarkable individual living in Manchester for many years was William Sturgeon, the electrician, he was born under circumstances as unfavourable as can well be imagined for scientific culture, and spent many years as a private soldier in the Artillery; yet, self-taught, he acquired such a knowledge of French, German, and Italian as enabled him to read scientific works in all these languages. In Dr. Angus Smith's "Centenary "of Science in Manchester" is given a list of fifty more or less important memoirs written by him, most of them on magnetic and electrical subjects. Dr. Joule has shown that Sturgeon was unquestionably the originator of the electro-magnet as well as the constructor of the first rotary magnetic engine. Dr. Joule says of him : "It may be doubted whether, "with the single exception of Dalton, the Scientific "Society of Manchester has ever experienced a severer

G

" calamity than Sturgeon's death." In 1845 came the terrible potato disease, which led to so many political and social changes ; various committees, on several of which I sat, were selected out of the scientific circles of Manchester to investigate its causes and remedies. Much good work was done in connection with the preservation of the tubers after they were taken out of the ground, but I now know that the time had not yet arrived for discovering and remedying the causes of the mischief. It was only at the close of the year when the potatoes were dug up that the prevalence of the disease was discovered, but the harm had been done in the early summer. Botanists were not familiar with the life-history of the Fungus Peronospora infestans, which attacked and destroyed the green aërial parts of the plant in the young state, and prevented the formation of the starch grains, which ought to have filled the cells of the tubers but which did not, because it had been thus destroyed.

During the fourth decade of this century the subject of clairvoyance had been much discussed in social circles, and in the early days of my professional life two men who lectured on the subject visited Manchester. The first of these was a Frenchman, who illustrated his lecture by experiments on a young woman. At one of his lectures the girl was declared to be in a state of sound sleep. A considerable number of medical men were present, including our leading ophthalmist, Mr. Wilson, and one Mr. Braid. The latter gentleman was loud in his denunciation of the entire affair. The audience then called upon Mr. Wilson for his opinion of the exhibition. Of course the question was, Is this exhibition an honest one or is it a sham ? Is the girl really asleep, or is she only pretending to be so ? In reply to the call of the audience, Mr. Wilson stood up and said : "The whole affair is as complete "a piece of humbug as I ever witnessed." The indignant lecturer, not familiar with English slang phrases, excitedly replied, "The gentleman says it "is all *Bog;* I say it is not *Bog;* there is no *Bog* in "it at all." By this time several of us, including Mr. Wilson, had gone upon the platform to examine the girl. I at once raised her eyelids, and found the pupils contracted to two small points. I called Wilson's attention to this evidence of sound sleep, and he at once gave me a look and a low whistle, conscious that he was in a mess. Braid then tested the girl by forcing a pin between one of her nails and the end of her finger. She did not exhibit the slightest indication of feeling pain, and Braid soon arrived at the conclusion it was not all *"Bog."* He subsequently commenced a long series of elaborate experiments, which ended in his placing the subject on a more philosophical basis than had been done by any of his predecessors.

For the term animal magnetism and other popular phrases Braid substituted " Hypnotism " and "Mono-"ideaism."

The hypothesis which he adopted was, that the subjects of these experiments required to have their mental faculties concentrated upon one idea; this accomplished, two effects will be produced in a few moments. The first is a state of sound sleep; which he succeeded in obtaining through either of the several senses, sight, hearing or touch; but his favourite plan was to seat the individual operated upon in an armchair, whilst he held a bright silver object, usually his lancet case, a few inches above the person's eyebrows, and required him to raise his eyes upwards until he saw the shining metal, soon after doing which, the patient went off into a sound sleep. But a still more remarkable result followed, indicating a condition of mind not so easily explained as illustrated.

On one occasion I called Braid in to see a young lad who had been suffering fearfully from a succession of epileptic attacks, which had failed to yield to medicinal treatment. So far as the epilepsy was concerned the hypnotic treatment was a perfect success; the boy after having long endured numerous daily attacks, was perfectly relieved after the third day's hypnotic operation. For five subsequent years, during which the youth remained under my observation, the epilepsy did not return. Braid always awoke his subjects from their hypnotic condition by sharply clapping his hands close to the sleepers' ears, which at once aroused them.

One day before doing this, Braid said to me,

" I will now show you another effect of hypnotism.
" Lend me your pocket-book and pencil." I did so.
He then placed the book in the boy's left hand,
which he raised into a convenient position in front
of the lad's breast. My pencil was placed in his
right hand, which was lifted into such a position that
the point of the pencil rested upon one of the pages
of the book. This attitude was rigidly maintained
until Braid whispered in his ear, " Write your name
" and address." The lad did so. " John Ellis,
" Lloyd Street, Manchester." This done, the book
and pencil were restored to my pocket. Braid then
awoke the boy and asked, " John, what were you
" doing just now " ? He looked about rather wildly
for a moment, and persistently answered, " Nothing."
Braid then sent him off to sleep again. The question
was again asked, " John, what were you doing just
" now " ? The lad answered promptly, but in a low
voice, " Writing my name and address." A
succession of similar experiments clearly indicated
two things ; first, that a mesmerised individual would
do what he was told to do ; second, that things done
when in that state were remembered only when
the same condition was resumed ; otherwise they
were forgotten, indicating a dual state of mind,
which, so far as I know, has not yet been
satisfactorily explained. I cannot learn that Braid's
method of experimental inquiry and of philosophical
induction has been continued by any person since he
died.

The second visitor to Manchester was of a different type. He appeared to be a man of some financial position in the world, since he had a gentlemanly demeanour and kept a yacht, of which a lad whom he brought with him to Manchester was said to be cabin-boy. It was affirmed that this lad was a clairvoyant, who could see to read, however much his eyes were plastered up. Some persons were invited out of the audience to apply this plastering, and after they had done so, the lad certainly read as easily as before. I at once expressed myself dissatisfied with the test, and was requested by some of the audience to undertake the closing of the eyes with these plasters. I tried to do so, but careful watching convinced me that by vigorous movements of the muscles acting upon the eyelids, the lad contrived to loosen a minute fold of the plaster close to his eye; through this fold he managed to read the books. I saw at once this could be stopped, by cutting a long strip of plaster which should cover the eyebrows, and at the same time bind down the edges of all the plasters with which the eyes were closed. In order to prevent any muscular action from disturbing this additional bandage, I stretched it tightly round the temples and fastened the two ends firmly together at the back of his head. I had no sooner done this with one of his eyes, than he prevented me from adopting the same plan with the other; he began to yell and declared I was killing him with pain. His master instantly turned upon me, and affirmed that I had covered that part of the lad's forehead with which he did see. Then the credulous fools in the audience fell foul of me for being so cruel. Of course I threw the thing up and resumed my seat. The next day a few medical friends met the two fellows at their hotel and plugged each of the boy's eyes with small balls of cobbler's wax; the clairvoyant's vision at once terminated, they left, and no more was afterwards heard of them.

CHAPTER VI

YOUNG medical men, however successful, have
usually a considerable amount of leisure time; and
such was my own case. Gradually this time was
spent in more and more definite scientific research.
Whilst a student in London, I had been treated with
the greatest kindness by most of the professors. I
was intimate with Lindley, through my long-continued
labour for the "Fossil Flora of Great Britain," of which
he was one of the two editors. I was also in the
habit of associating with Dr. Sharpey at the meetings of the Royal Society and at the soirées of the
Marquis of Northampton. At the time referred to,
Sharpey had just published a new edition of the best
student's text-book, known as "Quain's Anatomy."

Amongst other points with which he had enriched this edition were some extended notes on the structure and development of bones. The publication by the Sydenham Society of an English translation of the two works of Schwann and Schleiden on the cell question had brought that subject prominently before British physiologists. It had long been known that certain minute cavities called *lacunæ* were abundant in most, or rather as was believed then to be the case in all bones ; and the question which arose was—Did these lacunæ originate in cells ? In 1842, I amused myself during my vacant hours in making some thin sections of the bones of quadrupeds, with a view to throwing light on the debated problem. These early investigations led to others in 1848–50, which will be noticed further on, when I shall have to call attention to the importance of the two works just named.

A little later, my friend Mr. Sidebotham and I were stimulated by the researches of Mr. Ralfs of Penzance, to study practically the lower Confervaceæ, the Desmideæ, and the Diatomaceæ. Spending one evening together over these studies, my friend showed me a small slide which he had received from Mr. Reckitt of Boston, containing some beautiful diatoms in a marine sediment from the Levant. Examining these slides in search of diatoms, my eye fell upon an object which made me spring out of my chair. It was a perfect specimen of a marine Foraminifer, the shell of which was perforated by numerous large and conspicuous examples of the Foramina, to which the group owes its name of "Foraminifera." I had already obtained a translation of Ehrenberg's original memoirs on the formation of chalk, in which work similar specimens were figured; but this was the first real one that I had seen. I at once put myself in communication with Mr. Reckitt, of Boston, from whom Mr. Sidebotham had received the above specimen. That gentleman forwarded to me a small supply of the Levant mud, every grain of which I carefully preserved in a series of microscopic slides, and at once began to make drawings of the characteristic objects which these slides contained. I soon found myself on the threshold of an important investigation, and promptly threw my old "Culpepper" overboard, and mustered courage to purchase one of Dancer's best microscopes. Whether for good or for evil, I was obviously drawn into a current of microscopic investigation, which brought along with it a large circle of scientific correspondents, who, knowing the work on which I was engaged, supplied me with materials for examination from various quarters of the globe. I was especially thus aided by Professor Bailey, of the Military College of West Point, U.S.; by Charles Darwin, who had just returned from his South American investigations; Mr. Ralfs, the micro-botanist; Mr. Edward Charles Worth; Drs. Carpenter and Mantell; and Mr. Harris, of Charing, in Kent. The result was the production of a memoir

in 1847, published in Vol. VIII. of "Transactions of
"the Literary and Philosophical Society of Man-
"chester," with the title of "Some of the Microscopic
"Objects Found in Mud of the Levant, and other
"Deposits, with Remarks on the Mode of Formation
"of Calcareous and Infusorial Siliceous Rocks." This
memoir was so well received by the scientific world
that I almost felt an obligation resting on me to
carry still further a series of similar investigations.
I received complimentary letters from Darwin, Murchison, W. B. Carpenter, Professor J. Phillips, and
a host of other naturalists, who seemed to assume
that I should go further into the subject; and in
1848 I resumed the study of Foraminifera, my
knowledge of which was further increased by two
incidents. I should, in passing, remark that attention was not now being drawn to the Foraminifera
for the first time. Lamarck had long ago figured the
fossil forms so abundant in the Calcaire Grossier of
the Paris basin. At the end of the last century,
Soldarii had published a large number of remarkable
figures of recent forms; whilst in more modern times
D'Orbigny, though, like all his predecessors, misled
by the idea of their nautiloid affinities, was diligently
studying their varied forms.

A ship belonging to my father was chartered for
the Danube, to bring back a cargo of corn. I
instructed the captain to miss no opportunity of
obtaining for me samples of the bed of the Ægean
Sea. He was not unsuccessful in the materials

which he brought back. I found it rich in Foraminifera, especially in the finest forms of Polystomella
crispa. During the first three decades of the century, the Foraminifera had been regarded as the
internal shells of a small Cephalopodous mollusc.
In my memoir on the Levant mud, I ignorantly
allowed myself to be led by Ehrenberg, who believed
them to be Bryozoa, closely related to the genera
Flustra and Eschara.

The specimens now accumulating in my hands
soon showed me that this was a mistake. Whilst
my own experience was thus altering my views, I
learnt that, some time previously, Dujardin had been
investigating some living forms of Foraminifera ;
which observations made it clear, that in them at
least the soft animal was little more than a structureless jelly or animated slime, like that forming the
body of the well-known Proteus animalcule, but
capable of protruding filaments of great tenuity,
through the Foraminifera thin shells. This, which
proved to be the true explanation of the organisation
of these animals, had been before the Académie des
Sciences in 1835. But as yet nothing was known
of the structure of their shells. My rich supply of
Polystomella enabled me in beginning with them to
throw light on this question of structure. The
results of my inquiry were announced in a memoir
published in the second volume of the " Transactions
" of the London Microscopical Society." My conclusions respecting the soft animal now approximated

closely, on the whole, to those arrived at by M. Dujardin.

At a later period I investigated the shells of other Foraminifera by preparing microscopic sections from them, and in this way I showed that whilst the organisation of the living slimy animal was as low as it well could be, the structure of many of their shells was as complicated as it was beautiful.

At a somewhat later date Carpenter carried on a series of investigations, in which he adopted the same methods, and arrived at similar conclusions. The second of the two incidents to which I have referred, though different, led to equally important results.

My correspondent, Mr. Reckitt of Boston, had made the discovery, that wells sunk a little deeper than usual reached a wide spread layer of sea sand, showing that at a geologically very recent period the waters of the Wash had flowed much more deeply and broadly inland than had hitherto been known to be the case. Specimens of a deep layer of sand obtained in a similar way demonstrated that the land on that side of the great Norfolk estuary had been under water. Samples of the sand from these two opposite localities furnished me with a rich harvest of beautiful foraminiferous shells, the study of which led to new and not unimportant results. In the latter part of the last century a writer of the name of Walker established a small genus of minute flask-shaped shells, under the name of Lagena.

On receiving a liberal supply of the Boston shells from Mr. Reckitt, I tried an experiment that proved so successful that I adopted it ever afterwards when separating the more minute Foraminifer shells, from the ooze dredged up from the deeper seas. The material was first thoroughly dried before a fierce fire, and then rapidly stirred up in a broad-mouthed vessel filled with cold water. The result was that the chambered cavities of the Foraminiferous shells, being now full of air, floated to the surface, whilst a gentle stirring with the hand soon sent all the particles of sand and mud to the bottom. The surface residue was now floated off into a shallow dish and allowed to dry. On examining the material thus obtained from the Boston sand, I found that it almost wholly consisted of a mass of beautiful and varied pieces of Foraminiferous shells. I further discovered that the aggregation was especially rich in examples of Walker's genus, Lagena. Walker had already seen and given names to about five of these objects. After a minute study of my specimens I prepared a memoir, in which they were figured and described. But the study of these objects led me to an important conclusion, which I discovered at a later period to be applicable to the entire group of the Foraminifera. I demonstrated that such was their capacity for variation at different ages and from different localities, that long strings of genera and species might be arranged in linear series, rendering it possible that all the series might be regarded as mere varieties of one species.

All these conclusions will be found in my paper in the January number of the *Magazine of Natural History* for 1848. But another procedure was now suggested. In 1848 Dr. William Carpenter had been investigating the structure of some fossil Nummulites, also Foraminifera from the Tertiary beds of South-Western France, after which he also turned his attention to some of the recent Foraminifera, and it was recommended that he and I should combine our observations and conjointly produce some elaborate work on the Foraminifera; the final conclusion arrived at was that I should prepare a monograph on the recent Foraminifera of Great Britain, and that he should produce a volume on the general study of the Foraminifera. This plan was carried out, and my volume was published by the Ray Society in 1857, and Carpenter's was issued by the same society in 1862.

Meanwhile various other interesting points were attracting my attention. About this time I sent to the Yorkshire Philosophical Society a short memoir entitled " On the Scaly Vegetable Heads or "Collars from Runswick Bay supposed to belong to "the 'Zamia gigas.'" This memoir was published in the " Proceedings " of the Society, and the subject still in 1894 continues to excite considerable interest as well as a large amount of dispute as to its nature and affinities. In 1822, Young of Whitby had published two figures (plate 2, fig. 6) and (plate 3, fig. 7) of a flowerlike fossil identical with that which I described in my York memoir. Young's figures had attracted no especial attention until 1834, when my father collected further and finer specimens of the same objects. In 1835 I had gone down to Runswick Bay, from which the fossils had been obtained, to see if I could get new examples of these remarkable organisms, which I had succeeded in doing. But as yet no definite conclusion could be arrived at respecting their nature. My friend, the late Mr. James Yates, F.G.S., also obtained a fine series of the same objects, which he ultimately sold to the Geological Museum of the Jardin des Plantes of Paris, where the specimens now are. Shortly after the publication of the above mentioned brief communication by the Yorkshire Society, I wrote a much more detailed and liberally illustrated one for one of the London societies, but which somehow fell into the hands of the celebrated botanist, Robert Brown. This memoir had subsequently an eventful history. Brown was so cautious a man that he left behind him when he died a mass of drawings and memoranda that ought to have been published years previously. In the hands of such a man my memoir had no chance. In it I had figured and described all the specimens within my reach that were calculated to throw light on the morphology and botanical affinities of the objects, the conclusion at which I had permanently arrived being identical with that

announced in the York memoir, viz., that the objects
were part of the fructification of some Cycadean
plant. The rocks in which my specimens had been
obtained were crowded with the Cycadean fronds of
Zamia gigas and I occasionally discovered fragments
of Cycadean stems in the same strata; but all this
was much too hypothetical to satisfy the cautious
Robert Brown. He did not recommend the publication of the memoir, which was then returned to me.
Not satisfied with this, I sent the communication to
my friend Edward Forbes, then a rising star in the
scientific circles of the metropolis. He wrote to me
acknowledging the receipt of my paper, but I heard
no more about it for several months. Tired of
waiting so long and fruitlessly, I wrote to Forbes,
inquiring what he proposed to do with the memoir,
when I received from him a most penitent letter.
He said again that he had received my packet, and
that he had at once put it in some safe place, but
that he had never afterwards been able to discover
where that place was. Years rolled by before I heard
anything more of my MS., but I learnt from others
that such was the state of confusion in Forbes' study
and library, that the prospect of its recovery was hopeless. I then abandoned the subject and turned my
attention to other matters; but having begun this
narrative I may as well jump over a few years to record
the ultimate development of the story. Forbes died in
1854. A letter soon afterwards reached me from
one of his executors, stating that they had found

amongst a mass of other papers some documents
that appeared to belong to me, and wishing to know
what they must do with them. They were soon sent
to me; but, sick and weary of the whole affair, I thrust
the packet into a drawer and almost forgot its
existence. In the autumn of 1867 I saw a short
paragraph in the *Athenæum*, announcing that
Mr. Carruthers of the British Museum was engaged
upon the study of the British Fossil Cycadeæ, and
would be much obliged for the receipt of any information on the subject that could be supplied to him.

Though not knowing Mr. Carruthers personally, I
wrote telling him of my unfortunate memoir, and
offering to place text and plates at his disposal, to be
used in any way that he might think fit. In reply,
he informed me that he would shortly be passing
through Manchester and would call upon me. He
did so, and I gave all my documents unreservedly
into his hands. He then informed me that he was
on his way to Scarborough and Whitby to study the
very objects described and figured on my memoir,
and now to his surprise found that I was engaged
upon the work that he had contemplated doing. He
further informed me that he had obtained a grant
from the Linnæan Society in aid of the investigation ;
and that if I placed my memoir in his hands he
would undertake that it should be published along
with his own, without my having any further
trouble. All this was done, and amongst other
Cycadean genera that Mr. Carruthers was creating,

he introduced my specimens under the generic
name of " Williamsonia." But even yet my un-
happy memoir was not beyond the reach of trouble.
For economical reasons the officials of the Linnæan
Society left out of their plates some of the figures
which I had introduced into mine. This change
was forgotten when the proofs were corrected, the
result being that when I received my copies of the
memoir I discovered that the figures and letters of
reference on the plates and those in the text were
in hopeless disagreement. This was indeed a memoir
doomed to disaster.

Similar objects to those described in it have since
been found in Sweden and India and other parts of
the globe, and are now included under the same
generic name. Opinions have varied as to the group
of plants in which the " Williamsonia " ought to be
placed, but at the present time (1894) the pendu-
lum, after swinging hither and thither, has returned
to my own original idea, that these objects are
Cycadean.

But whilst the investigations here recorded were
in project a purely botanical question was also
engaging my attention. One of the most lovely of
the forms of aquatic life is the minute, fairy-like
sphere known as *Volvox globator*, familiar to all
microscopists. This object had been discovered by
Leeuwenhoek so far back as 1699, but for a century
and a half little, if any, addition had been made to our
knowledge of these elegant organisms, beyond what

was bequeathed to us by its original discoverer. As late as the days of Ehrenberg and even of Professor Rupert Jones (1847) it was still a debated question whether the object was a plant or an animal, both of the above observers having accepted the latter of these conclusions.

So far as its appearance was concerned, the little structure was a very thin walled, delicate, transparent sphere, to the inner surface of which a large number of minute symmetrically arranged green specks were adherent. A number of tightly drawn threads, delicate as the spiders' web employed by astronomers, extended from each green point to those that immediately surrounded it. Besides these features, from four to six globes, each larger than the green specks, but varying exceedingly in size and appearance in different specimens, either floated free in the colourless fluid that filled the cavity of the parent object, or adhered to the inner surface of the pellucid wall of the sphere. After weeks of patient observation under the microscope, I one day caught a momentary glimpse of a few symmetrical hexagonal areolæ on the inner surface of the pellucid wall. It appeared but for a moment, but during that moment it was sufficiently distinct to convince me that it was part of some structural peculiarity that had hitherto escaped observation. I at once devoted time to the recovery of the vision, but for weeks I laboured in vain. I then tried the experiment of allowing a number of the objects to soak for some

time in a solution of iodine and glycerine, and in a
few of the organisms thus treated I obtained what I
was in search of, and which gave me a clue to the
structural history of the Volvox.

I found that this hexagonal object had originated
from one of the numerous minute green points
already referred to. It began to enlarge, becoming
conspicuous among its smaller neighbours. It next
split into two, then into four, until a succession of
such binary divisions produced a spherical cluster of
green protoplasm enclosed within a delicate transparent sphere. At first these subdivided atoms
adhered closely one to another; at length the divisions ceased, but the sphere continued to enlarge,
became hollow, and eventually the green objects
arranged themselves in a single layer surrounding
the central cavity, yet adhering to each other by their
thin margins. This absolute contact of each protoplasm with its neighbours became interrupted except
at five or six points. As this interrupted continuity
increased, each protoplasm ceased to retain its
homogeneous condition ; it separated into two elements. The small green mass became suspended in
a transparent colourless fluid, the two elements now
becoming enclosed within a delicate colourless cell
wall. The further enlargement of each of the
cells thus produced caused the five or six points of
mutual contact to become drawn out into the delicate
threads already referred to. The little compound
sphere next became detached from the inner surface

of the wall of the parent Volvox, to which it had thus far firmly adhered, and floated free in the interior of the older organism, along with four or five others similarly developed. Finally the parent structure broke up, liberating the young forms, each of which then became the parent of a succeeding generation.

This series of observations not only demonstrated that Volvox was a plant, but it has since been made the type of a cryptogamic group, now recognised as the Volvocineæ. But though I thus succeeded in laying the foundation of a scientific treatment of this lovely object in 1851–52, more had yet to be done before we obtained a fuller knowledge of its remarkable history. Stein and my old friend Professor Cohn, of Breslau, brought to light many important facts connected with its sexuality; yet we are still far from knowing all about it. It is evident that Volvox is subject to some change equivalent to an alternation of generations, apparently dependent upon changes in the seasons, as well as upon other changes in its surroundings. The boundaries of the species are far from determined, notwithstanding what Klein has recently done in that direction. These objects still attract by their fairy-like aspect, and they have now become more interesting because of the remarkable morphological and physiological phenomena which what we know of their life-history has already revealed.

CHAPTER VII

Resumption of cell question—Ossification of cartilage—
Professor Schwann and Dr. Schleiden—Dr. Sharpey
and bone development—Agassiz' classification of fishes
—Geological distribution of four classes—Bearing of
Ganoid scales on Owen's " Odontology"—Memoir for
Royal Society in 1849—Second memoir for the Royal
Society 1850—Professor Kölliker—Position of oral teeth
in relation to skeleton — Oral teeth really dermal
structure—Huxley's acceptance of this—Mr. Charles
Tomes—Structure of fish bones—Links in scale of
organisation missing from living forms but found in
fossils—Links in bones of living fishes and placoid saw
fish.

WHILST these various works were in progress,
another interesting subject was occupying my mind.
During my medical studies at the London University, the Professor of Physiology, Dr. Sharpey, had,
as I have already observed, called my attention to
some moot questions connected with the structure
and development of the bones of the human skeleton.
I had never wholly lost sight of this subject, and about
the time of which I am now writing I began to give
it more serious and systematic attention. But before

saying anything of the results of these investigations, it will be well to give some preliminary explanation, and this explanation is the more desirable since biological science has just undergone a most remarkable development, which has placed most students of life and organisation in a wholly new position.

In the very youngest state of all the mammalia, including man, almost every bone is represented by a cartilage, or what is familiarly known as gristle. This cartilage consists of a more or less flexible and structureless substance, in which are lodged numerous clusters of minute hollow spheres, known as cells, and each of these undeveloped bones is invested by a closely adherent thin layer of membrane known, in the earliest stages of growth when the future bone is still cartilaginous, as " perichondrium," but later on, when hard bony matter becomes formed, as " periosteum." The first earthy matter deposited in the bone accumulates in the structureless parts of the cartilage between the clusters of cells. This first process of ossification is soon followed by another, in which the thin membrane referred to as " perichondrium " also becomes hardened by phosphate of lime being deposited in its substance.

This perichondrium is now replaced by a new layer of membrane like its predecessor, but which, having now a layer of true bone beneath it, is designated " periosteum." I have called these two forms of bony matter by names which I shall directly have to use. That formed in the cartilage I have called "chondriform " bone, and that in the more external layers of membrane, "membraniform" bone. In the mammalia, nearly, but not quite, all the former tissue disappears at a very early age, the growth of the skeleton being effected by the addition and subsequent ossification of layer after layer of periosteum.

Minute cavities, called lacunæ, abound in each layer of membraniform bone, in all mammalia and reptiles. The question of the origin of these lacunæ brings before us a remarkable epoch in the history of biology, viz., the fourth decade of the present century. Previously to that date the subject of the unity of the organic world was altogether misunderstood. Thus, prior to the period referred to, it was supposed that the development and growth of animal bodies were brought about by processes wholly different from those which produced the same results in the vegetable world, an error which led to endless vague speculations and baseless guesses. Much was gained when thinkers arrived at the sound conclusions of *omne vivum ex viva* and *omne vivum ex ovo*. Both these axioms struck at the root of the nonsense prevalent under the name "Spontaneous Generation."

But a still greater end was attained when we learnt the signification of the abiding axiom of *omne vivum ex cellulâ*. Then it was that we understood for the first time the true seat of life and its uninterrupted transmission from generation to generation.

In 1839 Professor Schwann, of the University of
Louvain, brought out his renowned work, "Micro-
"scopical Researches into the Accordance in Struc-
"ture and Growth of Animals and Plants." A little
previously, Dr. Schleiden, the Professor of Botany
in the University of Jena, published a collection of
papers, in which the cells and cell development seen
in the vegetable world were industriously investigated, and, at the same time, Mirbel and others were
occupied with similar researches. Thus the extreme
importance of the cell in the life-history of plants
and animals soon became known and universally
recognised.

A cell is a minute atom of a semi-fluid substance
that may or may not be invested by a "cell wall,"
which is in the first instance an extremely thin
membrane. The contents of the cell are of a com-
posite character, and with varying characteristics,
though in the young state chiefly composed of what
is designated protoplasm. This compound element
can, and frequently does, remain for a long time in
active vitality, without being invested by a cell wall.
The latter is an effect of the vital activity of the
protoplasm, not its cause, but in most cases it is the
usual effect of that life.

We now know that all the tissues alike of the
animal and of the plant have been produced by the
action of these cells. This truth was only realised
by biologists very slowly. Consequently, when Dr.
Sharpey first called my attention to the question of

bone development, he was not prepared to recognise that each of the minute lacunæ of bone was the product of a single cell, though there were other microscopists who accepted that explanation. It was this, along with various similar uncertainties, that led me to pursue my own investigations into the development of bones and teeth. I commenced by making microscopic sections of some of the mammalian quadrupeds, but discovered nothing beyond what had already been done by Dr. Sharpey. I then turned to bones, teeth, and scales of fishes, both recent and fossil, from which I obtained much more valuable and interesting results. I began by preparing microscopic sections of a large number of fossil scales, in some of which I found structures of remarkable beauty and interest.

M. Agassiz on commencing his celebrated researches amongst the fossil fishes of the world found that the existing classifications of living forms were inapplicable to the fossil ones. Hence he proceeded to construct a new one better adapted to his object. He established four groups based upon peculiarities in the structure of their scales. These were the Ganoids, Placoids, Cycloids, and Ctenoids.

The Ganoids were the most highly organised of these classes. In them the scales were rhomboidal in form, thick and hard in substance, and, moreover, had their outer surface covered with a layer of bright, shining enamel. Few fishes now living belong to this group, but it is well represented by the huge

Lepidasteus, or bony pike of the Mississippi and other of the larger rivers of America, and by the Polypterus, a smaller type found in the River Nile. But these Ganoid forms are most abundant in a fossil state, more especially in the strata older than the chalk. The second class, or Placoids, are much more widely represented at the present day, and are also comparatively abundant in all the strata from the clay down to the Devonian rocks. This group contains all the tribes of sharks and skates and rays. These are specially characterised by having their skins studded thickly with those enormously sized teeth commonly known as shagreen and used as a covering for cases of compasses and other similar instruments. These fishes have no proper scales beyond these dermal or skin teeth.

The Cycloids and Ctenoids comprehend most of the ordinary fishes, with which every one is familiar. The scales of the Cycloids have the upper surface of each scale marked with a series of concentric ridges, which are parallel with the margin of each scale.

The Ctenoids have scales of which the anterior part is identical with those of the Cycloids, but at the posterior part each concentric ridge terminates in one or more minute spines pointed backwards.

The scales of the Ganoids furnished some remarkable results ; each scale presented three layers, a lower one of bone, usually with magnificent lacunæ ; a middle one composed of true tooth structure, and an upper one of shining enamel.

When Owen, in his " Odontography," published his notions respecting the way in which the dentine or tubulated substance of the human tooth was developed, he described a very elaborate system of soft structures, by means of which this dentine was produced. Identical tissues are produced in the middle layer of these scales by much simpler methods. A layer of thin membrane, which by calcification in the *basal part* of the scale is converted into bone, ascends into a higher portion of that scale, and being calcified, is there converted into tooth substance. Recent observations demonstrate that the dentine of the human tooth is produced in an equally simple way. My discovery of the simple mechanism by which the formation of tooth structures in fishes was produced, now proves to be equally applicable to all teeth.

The results of these investigations were laid before the Royal Society in June 1849, and published in Part II. of the " Philosophical Transactions " for that session. The same memoir dealt with the dermal teeth of the shagreen or skins of the sharks and rays, collectively designated by Agassiz the Placoid fishes.

I devoted my leisure hours during the remainder of 1849 and the first half of 1850 to a similar study of the Cycloid and Ctenoid fishes, but I also extended my researches into the structure and development of the bones, as well as of the integumental appendages of these animals. My results were embodied in a second memoir, read before the Royal Society in 1850 and published in Part II. of the " Philosophical Transactions " for 1851.

These two memoirs enunciate several new truths, sufficiently important, indeed, to bring Professor Kölliker, the distinguished anatomist of Würtzburg, to Manchester, with the object of studying the specimens from which my new conclusions were drawn, and with nearly all of which he cordially agreed. In past years there had been much discussion respecting the relationships which the human and other mammalian teeth bore to the skeletons with which they were associated.

My investigations among the scales and teeth of fishes led me to the conclusion that these dermal scales and oral teeth were identical, or rather, what are technically called homologous organs; in other words, that teeth belonged to the skin and not to the skeleton. This novel and unexpected determination was speedily accepted by Huxley.

The absolute truth of this determination was afterwards demonstrated by Mr. Charles Tomes, the eminent dental surgeon. That gentleman investigated the origin of oral teeth in the dog-fish, a close ally of the shark, and the shagreened skin of which is one mass of minute dermal teeth. He showed that in a very young condition of these fishes a fold of the shagreened skin extended round the lip and entered the mouth; certain of the dermal teeth thus introduced became planted upon the several oral bones, where they gradually developed into ordinary oral teeth of that class of fishes.

These views, already adopted by Huxley and Kölliker, were alike based upon my discoveries of what took place in fishes' scales, and their recognition as the representation of teeth.

Whilst pursuing the above investigation, and especially keeping in view the question of the origin of the lacunæ of bone, I made the discovery that a large number of fishes contained no lacunæ, though in others they were abundant. The same research also brought prominently to light further facts. I found that in many of the so-called cartilaginous fishes—*i.e.*, sharks and rays—only one kind of bone exists, which is produced by deposit in the intercellular spaces of the cartilage, of which all bones primarily consist, and of a phosphate of lime, which gives additional firmness to the skeleton. Bone thus formed I designate *chondriform* bone. Amongst the ordinary bones of fishes I discovered two forms of bone—an inner one of chondriform type growing inwards, and an outer one deposited in the successively superadded layers of the periosteum, on the membranous layer with which all mammalian bones are invested. Successive layers of this membrane were added to the pre-existing ones so long as the period of the animal's growth continued, the pre-existing ones becoming calcified, and thus adding to the thickness of all of what I designated *membraniform* bones. My two terms are practically identical with the *ecderon* and *enderon* suggested by Huxley at a somewhat later period. Mine were based upon the two soft tissues, cartilage, and membrane with which the mineral substance became organically united. Huxley's were based upon the two opposite directions in which the two processes of calcification extended themselves; the first outwardly and the second inwardly, each starting from a line to which our author gave the name of "protomorphic." The most interesting of my discoveries were based upon the various modes in which these two forms of bone growth arranged themselves amongst the different types of fishes. Few educated persons, in these days of Darwinian thought, are ignorant of the fact that, alike in the animal and vegetable kingdoms, life presents a succession of forms from the lowest to the highest types. Not that all the links of these chains are living now. Vast numbers of them existed only during the immeasurable ages of the past, of these we only obtain glimpses here and there, through the labours of the geologist and the palæontologist.

By turning my attention alike to recent and fossil forms of bone, scale, and tooth, I was able to fill in some links of their chain of organisation, which the living forms alone could not have taught. But even amongst the living animals we find a progression not only in entire races, but in individuals; and in each of these latter we find similar development in the successive stages of life dependent upon advance of age. Dealing with the

development of the skeleton of the vertebrate
animals from this point of view, progression mani-
fests itself conspicuously. In every case the production of chondriform bone indicates an earlier state of
organisation than membraniform bone does. Sharks
and rays, the placoid fishes of Agassiz, have long
been known as the cartilaginous fishes; but their
skeletons are not, as the name might imply, mere
unaltered cartilage; this tissue is converted into
chondriform bone. But in one of this tribe—the
sawfish—we find the bones of the snout flattened,.
immensely elongated, and carrying a row of the huge
teeth along each of its margins, to which the animal
owes its popular name. This powerful aggressive
organ would not be sufficiently rigid for its purpose
were it solely composed of chondriform bone. Such
bone is present in an inner layer, but a second layer
of exostial bone is added externally. This is formed
of a soft layer that is somewhat midway between
true membrane and cartilage, in which small verti-
cally disposed rods of hard tissue are developed
and packed tightly together, giving to the snout the
rigidity which it requires. Nature thus supplies her
own need out of her existing resources, subjecting
them only to such modifications as each case
demands. Anyhow, we have here a first trace of
an introduction of membraniform bone amongst the
cartilaginous fishes. We next advance to those
fishes in which the skeleton consists of chondriform
and true membraniform bone developed side by side..

I

Here the former is not, as in the higher animals, a mere temporary provision, but a permanent structure; and, lastly, we reach the higher mammalia, including man, in which the chondriform bone is abundantly developed in the early stages of life, but where it is a temporary scaffold, to be removed when the permanent membraniform bone is sufficiently strong to bear the weight of the superstructure. Even here, nature does not waste her materials: where two bones rub against each other at a large joint, as at the shoulder, the friction would soon produce mischief, were it not reduced to a minimum. Whilst the cartilage disappears elsewhere, a layer of it permanently covers the ends of the two bones, which meet, as at the shoulder-joint; and underlying this cartilage, as Sharpey was the first to notice, we find, permanently, a small amount of chondriform bone.

The above two memoirs, the objects of which I have endeavoured to make intelligible, effected my election to the Fellowship of the Royal Society, June 1854.

CHAPTER VIII

Death of Owens—Announcement of will—Proceedings of trustees—Theological question—Professors appointed—First meeting with Dr. Greenwood—Manchester Free Library—My own appointment to Chair of Natural History—Botany—Geology—Opening of college—My early teaching—Progress of college—Evening classes—Decrease in number of students—Condition of boys' education in Manchester—Resignation of Principal Scott—Appointment of Professor Greenwood to Principalship — Laboratory teaching needed — My Chair too big for good teaching to be possible—Professor Dawkins' appointment—Social life of professors — Difficulties of popularity.

ON August 1, 1846, the *Manchester Guardian* made the following obituary announcement: " On the 29th " ult., aged 55 years, John Owens, Esq. of Nelson " Street." This event proved, little as I was then aware of it, to be one affecting in a most important manner my future life. Glimpses of the possibility that such might be the case dawned upon me a few days later, when a leading article in the same newspaper announced that the deceased gentleman had left a very large amount* of property to be

* "The account was not finally closed until May 1857;

devoted to the establishment of a college in Manchester, the money "to be applied for the purposes
" of affording to youths of the age of fourteen years
" and upwards, instruction in the branches of educa-
" tion taught in the English universities, free from
" the religious tests which limit the extension of
" university education. The trustees for this pur-
" pose include the Mayor, Dean, and Parliamentary
" representatives of Manchester, with other gentle-
" men of local reputation and influence."* This
announcement suggested to my mind the possibility
of my becoming associated with the college. The
time at which this bequest was made was one
unfavourable to the realisation of all kinds of property ; hence, owing to the various difficulties referred
to and encountered by the executors and trustees
appointed by the will, a long time elapsed before
any observable steps were taken to carry out Owens'
intentions. From time to time the local newspapers gave broad hints to the gentlemen in whose
hands the estate was, that the outside world expected
them to move on a little more vigorously. The first
meeting of executors and trustees for educational

" and owing to accumulated interest, return of duties, and
" profitable investments in stocks, the total sum received
" by the trustees amounted to £96,942 1s. 1d. Of this sum
" upwards of £2000 was expended on college premises, law
" charges, and preliminary expenses."
    * Thompson's " Owens College, its Foundation and
" Growth."

purposes was not held until June 13, 1848. Some deaths had occurred meanwhile among persons named in the will, and the vacancies thus created had to be filled up. A committee of five of the members of the ruling body was appointed to consider the general features which were to characterise the new institution, both as regarded the subjects to be taught and the plans to be adopted, in order that such teaching should be most efficiently done. The gentlemen entrusted with this task considered the question of religious education. Their report was finally agreed upon in 1849, and was issued to the public in March 1850. This soon aroused a commotion, owing to the decision of the trustees to adopt the views of the committee on the question of religious teaching. They had concluded that no educational movement should be carried on without such religious instruction "as may elevate and " strengthen the moral and religious character of the " students, without encroaching upon the liberty of " conscience, which the testator has so anxiously " sought to protect." In a word, theological lectures should be delivered in the college, attendance on which by the students was to be voluntary. This decision speedily led to active opposition in the town. Both the *Guardian* and the *Examiner and Times* attacked it, the latter newspaper especially being most energetic in opposing " the in- " troduction of this theological wedge." On April 8, 1850, a meeting was held to consider whether the "proposed religious teaching in the Owen's "College be in accordance with the will and inten- "tion of its founder," and it was resolved that a deputation should be sent to the trustees on the subject. This was done on April 18, when strong objections were urged by the deputation to the views entertained by the trustees. On May 18, a counter deputation of Churchmen urged the trustees to adopt the teaching of theology in the college. But the question now assumed a legal aspect ; a "case" was submitted to two legal gentlemen, who decided in favour of the trustees. But the method finally adopted by these gentlemen was a very harmless one ; it was that a class should be established for the study of the Hebrew of the Old Testament, and a similar one for the Greek of the New ; besides which, a course of lectures was to be delivered by the Principal on the "Influence of Religion in Rela- "tion to the Life of the Scholar."

The appointment of the various professors now proceeded gradually. Dr. A. J. Scott was elected to the Principalship on October 23, 1850, Mr. Green- wood to the Classical Chair on November 19 of the same year.

Contemporaneously with this active college pre- paration Manchester townsmen were busied in dis- cussing the advantages of a Free Library. Being myself a member of this committee, I of course attended its meetings. Whilst sitting at one of them, a refined, delicate-looking young man entered the

room and took his place at the council table exactly
opposite to where I was sitting. A friend whispered
in my ear that the young stranger was Mr. Greenwood, the newly elected Professor of Classics. I was
candidate for the Chair of Natural History, but had
not received my appointment, neither was I in any
degree sure of obtaining the coveted chair. I need
scarcely add I regarded my *vis-à-vis* with considerable interest, not unmixed with envy of his
success. I was personally introduced to the young
man at the close of our meeting, which introduction proved to be the commencement of a friendship
of the closest type; a friendship that has lasted
until a month ago, when my beloved colleague
and Principal passed from here into eternity. I
little anticipated so important a result when I first
saw him enter that council room.

At the opening meeting of the said Free Library,
which, however, did not take place until September
1852, eighteen months after the opening of the
college, Sir James Stephen, Professor of Modern
History at Cambridge, said: " At Cambridge, as
" everywhere else, where educated men are brought
" together, Manchester is a name of deep and even of
" awful significance; for here is the metropolis of
" that Titanic industry, on the continued success of
" which England has deliberately pledged her station
" and her authority among the nations of the
" world."

My own appointment to the Professorship of

Natural History, which included Zoology, Botany, and Geology, was in January of 1851.

The college was opened March 12, 1851, by an address from Professor Greenwood on the languages and literature of Greece and Rome. Illness deferred the Principal's address until a later date. My own was delivered a few days after Mr. Greenwood's. The contemplation of the work that lay before me, that of teaching three subjects rolled into one, almost appalled me. But the first session closed before the end of its third month, being merely a provisional one, to enable the college to commence operations without further delay. Hence my brief course of lectures was confined to a hasty review of the animal kingdom. During the summer months I had time to deliberate on my plans. I decided to divide my course into two parts, dealing with the animal kingdom one year, and with botanical and geological subjects a second year. The botanical portion of my work was that for which I was the least prepared. At that time the great schools for teaching chemistry and advanced botany were mainly to be found in Germany, and of the German language I was utterly ignorant; hence I was at a great disadvantage in endeavouring to work up the subject. Still the difficulty was overcome by determination and work.

Reverting to the progress of the college, some circumstances of importance demand notice. During the first complete session, 1851-2, sixty-two students were scattered through the several classes. The number of regular day students rose in the sessions 1852–3 and 1853–4 to seventy-one.

So early as the year 1854, Professor Copley Christie and I applied for permission to open classes for the teaching of our respective subjects to working men in the evening. The trustees sanctioned our application, and the result of this first experiment of the utility of such teaching is shown by the fact, that our precedent has been followed ever since. In my natural history class, the number of evening students rose in 1855 to eighteen, and in 1860 to forty-one.

The session 1854–5 showed a small decrease in the number of day students. This decline continued until 1856–7, when they sank to thirty-three—little more than half the number with which we started in 1851–2. There was evidently something seriously wrong. One fact was unquestionable, school education in Manchester was at that time at a very low ebb; of course the schoolmaster of the day ridiculed this explanation; but it was a fact. The students were not prepared for those higher standards of education which a collegiate institution demanded, and below which its professors could not descend. The teachers of the schools retorted by declaring that we could not know anything about their teaching, because they were not such fools as to send their upper students to us. Ere long the truth of our assertions was plainly demonstrated. At that time, the local university examinations were becoming popular, and were being held in a number of the larger centres of population. At length one such was held in Manchester, and when the usual annual report of these examinations was published, Manchester stood at the bottom of the entire list.

But whilst our complaints respecting the low standard of Manchester educationists were thus justified, other influences equally unfavourable were at work. At that time an opinion prevailed widely amongst the merchants of the town, that if lads were to do any good, either to their masters or to themselves, they must enter the warehouses very early in life, *i.e.*, by the time they were fourteen ; and, having done so, they must undertake the most menial of the operations which were demanded by the business men of the day. That this conviction was then very widely spread, even among the most intelligent portion of the mercantile community, I know from my own personal association with many such. But while influences so unfavourable to the progress of the college undoubtedly affected our position, there remained other causes within the college itself not calculated to promote our success.

The trustees requested the professors to assist them with their views as to the causes of the threatened failure. Professor Frankland, who held the Chair of Chemistry, spoke out very freely, and said he thought the training was too exclusively

classical, fitted only for those students who sought
B.A. or M.A. degree. To this, and other reasons of
weight, he added two suggestions of distinct significance. One was that scientific teaching should be
put in a more prominent position than it then
occupied, and further, that there should be periodical
meetings of the teaching staff to discuss the internal
management of the college.*

The most influential of the original trustees were
undoubtedly men who attached more value to
classical than to scientific training, as the stipends
respectively awarded to the two classes of professors
sufficiently indicated. The Principal, Dr. Scott, was
a man of the highest intellectual culture, but there
was then small appreciation of, and no demand for,
this kind of culture among the hard-headed and
eminently practical men of Lancashire. Whilst they
honoured the intellectual strength of the Principal,
his was not the line in which they wished their sons
to be trained; hence he failed to gain their entire
confidence.

The concluding defect reported by Professor
Frankland was one severely felt by the science
professors; it was that they found much difficulty
in obtaining access to the Principal. The conviction that some change in the relations of Principal and Professor was necessary, led to a meeting of the latter body at the house of Professor
Frankland, where a resolution was adopted and

* Thompson, p. 157.

forwarded to the trustees, asking them to appoint a Deputy Principal, who should be required to be at the college through certain hours of the day, where he could be easily reached by such of the professors as required to consult with him. The meaning of this procedure on the part of the staff was doubtless understood by the Principal, who on May 28, 1857, resigned his office. Dr. Scott's resignation robbed Manchester of a man of rare culture, and his death a few months later is said to have taken from the world more Dantesque learning than was left behind. On July 24 of the same year, Professor Green-wood was appointed in his place. During the first year of the new Principal's control, the decline in the number of ordinary students was arrested ; and in the three succeeding years they rose respectively to forty, fifty-seven, and sixty-nine. But many other additions were needful before the college attained to its ultimate career of real success. Great educational changes were meanwhile taking place outside Owens College. On the Continent the oral teaching of science in lecture rooms was gradually becoming supplemented by the practical training only attainable in the laboratory. Liebig had long previously employed such a method of teaching chemistry at Giessen, and had attracted students from many distant localities. Bunsen followed this example at Heidelberg, and with similar results. When Dr. Frankland was appointed to the Chemical Chair at Owens, he was provided with a laboratory, but a

long time elapsed before any other department of
the college was similarly favoured, yet natural
philosophy, engineering, and natural history in all
its departments required similar provision. Meanwhile the Manchester community began to discover
the advantages of a higher intellectual and scientific
training as preparation for even a commercial and
manufacturing life ; hence the authorities said an
extension of their teaching machinery was inevitable. I was one of the first of the teaching staff
to be affected by these changes. At the out-
set I had to teach comparative anatomy, botany,
geology, and palæontology. I saw that to make
the anatomy of lower animals intelligible, a knowledge of at least the broader features of human
anatomy was desirable ; that when, for instance,
I showed my students a few microscopic threads
given off from the intestine of an insect, and told
them that these were early representatives of the
kidney in higher animals, they should know what
this most highly developed organ was like. Still,.
although my need for a laboratory was so great,
there was no possibility of its being satisfied until
the college removed from its first home in Quay
Street to its present handsome buildings in Oxford
Road. This removal did not take place until
1872.

I soon found that to include this increased work in
a session of little more than eight months was almost
impossible, so I spread my complete course over two

sessions ; but at length even this system had to be abandoned.

The number of our students who sought the degrees of the London University steadily increased, and it became indispensable that my full course should be included in one session. Adequate teaching of so wide a range of subjects in so limited a period was an impossibility. Such a demand was too absurd to be credited, yet I was informed by the authorities that it must be done. The amount of my time required by the college was thus doubled, and the requisite leisure could only be obtained by abandoning some portion of my work elsewhere, and so I resigned my office of Surgeon to the Manchester Ear Institute. But the inevitable inadequacy of such hurried teaching compelled the council to obtain for me efficient relief, and in 1872 Mr. Boyd Dawkins was appointed lecturer in and subsequently Professor of Geology. This step, whilst on one hand it afforded the much needed relief, introduced me to a pleasant and lasting friendship.

Social life among the professors was very different in these earlier days of the college from anything possible now. As I have already stated, shortly after the college began its work we found the need of periodic meetings of its small staff. We arranged to hold them at our several houses in turn, on each fourth Saturday evening of the month. The early part of the meeting was devoted to business, the later hours to supper and sociality. This method of combining work with pleasure was continued by us for many years, indeed until the removal to the new buildings, when successive additions to the staff and consequent increase of time required for the business of the college, compelled us to abandon the home meetings and transfer them to the college buildings.

In the early years, when the staff consisted of only five or six professors, we were frequently invited in a body to the hospitable tables of the wealthy Manchester merchants. This social element in our life of hard work was extremely pleasant, and I believe that for many years the free intercourse between townsmen and staff succeeded in keeping down the town and gown feeling, so much to be deplored in University centres.

That by this time our teaching was become popular may be judged from one of the difficulties of our Principal, Dr. Greenwood. A merchant came into the Principal's room accompanied by his son. After explaining that he wanted the boy to be admitted as student, the Principal inquired which classes he would like his son to attend. The good merchant, jingling gold in his trousers' pockets with a proud consciousness he could afford it, replied, "Oh! I reckon he may tak' 'em all."

CHAPTER IX

M. Menière and Paris—Establishment of Ear Institute—
Fresh water animalculæ—Memoir in the *Journal of
Microscopical Science* — Birth and death of our first
child — Birth of other daughters and of a son —
Contributions to the *London Quarterly*—Journeys to
Switzerland with Mr. John Fernley—Removal to
Fallowfield—Construction of garden—Family excursion
through Switzerland—Illness and death of my wife.

LEAVING now the college and its progress for awhile,
I should like to glance at one or two incidents
which were of importance to me. During the early
college days I suffered from an attack of abscesses
of the glands of one of my ears. This was a
branch of surgery on which I had never received
any instruction; and on consulting some of the
leading surgeons of the town I discovered they
knew no more of the matter than I did. I resolved
to take some steps by which I could become better
acquainted with aural diseases. One of the most
eminent of European aural surgeons of those days
was Mons. Menière of Paris, surgeon to the celebrated Deaf and Dumb Hospital in the Rue de
St. Jaques. Being acquainted with Mons. Adolphe

Brongniart, the distinguished botanist and palæo-botanist, I wrote to ask him for an introduction to the eminent aurist. The result was that I received an extremely kind letter from M. Menière, inviting me to Paris, and offering to give me all the assistance in his power. I at once availed myself of his kindness, and spent day after day in his consulting-room.

I there studied his cases and became familiar with his instruments and the method of their employment. After this training I returned to London, where I received some further assistance and instruction from Mr. Toynbee and Mr. Harvey, then the two aurists of London, and I finally returned to Manchester to try how best to practise all I had learnt. I gathered together at my house a few influential friends to consult on the subject, and a resolution was adopted that we must establish an institution in Manchester for the treatment of aural diseases. My old friend, William Romaine Callender, afterwards one of the members for Manchester, suggested that he and I should together canvas the leading merchants of the district for subscriptions wherewith to support such an institution. We did so, and not wholly unsuccessfully. The Institution was established, and Sir James Bardsley, the leading local physician, accepted the office of president, and for long afterwards took the greatest interest in our scheme. A committee was formed. My brother-in-law, Mr. Bateson Wood,

K

undertook the office of secretary, and thus far our ship was launched. Of course it was my intention to be the medical officer of the new concern, but I had ascertained that there was a young medical man in the town who had paid some attention to aural ailments. He was an entire stranger to me; but I called upon him, introduced myself, explained our scheme and the extent of our arrangements, and invited him to co-operate with me as one of the surgeons to the Institute. This offer was accepted by him; he joined our committee, and we next proceeded to search for a local habitation. We found at the lower end of Oxford Street, near St. Peter's Square, a house that would serve our purpose. A day was fixed for commencing practical operations. When that day arrived I went to the Institute, wondering whether or not a single patient would make his or her appearance, and my heart rather sank when I found none. I sat down, however, to contemplate the situation, and shortly one man appeared. Whilst I was investigating his case and putting into practice my newly acquired knowledge, several other patients found their way into the waiting-room. After attending to all these, I returned home in elated spirits, fully assured our experiment was not going to end in failure. I continued to occupy the position of surgeon, along with my coadjutor Mr. McKeand, until, as I have previously stated, the college required all the time I could spare from private practice, and then I was compelled reluctantly to resign all connection with the Institution, though for many years I received aural patients at my own consulting-room.

Meanwhile, though professionally so fully occupied, natural science still interested me. A supply of the exquisite little fresh water animalculæ, the Melicerta ringens, made its appearance in a tank in which I was growing Vallisneria spiralis. This circumstance gave me the opportunity of submitting the animal to a careful study, which brought to light a number of points that had escaped the attention of previous observers. My resultant memoir was published in the *Quarterly Journal of Microscopical Science*. The ovary of the animal was sufficiently distinct, and I was able to watch the entire development of the ovum. When this became matured I desired to discover where and how it made its escape into the surrounding fluid, between which and it a considerable distance seemed to intervene. My first attempt to do so ended in a failure; after watching with my eye at the microscope a couple of hours, a professional summons called me away. My second attempt, though very wearisome, was successful. My eye never left the microscope through a long succession of hours. At length I saw the body of the transparent creature violently contorted, the egg passed through a very short oviduct into a long cloaca, by the complete eversion of which organ the ovum was set free. But my labours were not yet ended, though the painful retention of my eye at the microscope was not required to be so incessant. I succeeded in watching the successive changes which the yolk underwent during its conversion into an embryo, which latter moved freely for some time within its shell, but through which it ultimately broke and escaped into the surrounding water. Further changes were undergone by the creature before it attained the mature form; each of these was carefully observed and recorded, and at length I had the enjoyment of seeing my young nursling reach the full development of the parent form. After the publication of my memoir in January 1856, I received a communication from Mr. Pritchard, the well-known microscopist, and author of a copious volume on the Infusoria. He informed me that he was about to publish a new edition of this work, and was anxious to obtain my assistance. I eventually undertook to superintend the section which dealt with the systematic history of the Rotatoria and Rotiferæ. The new volume made its appearance in 1861.

Before, however, dwelling further upon these scientific observations, I will glance at a few domestic incidents of my comparatively unchequered life.

In 1845 our first child was born, but before she was four years old she was taken from us by whooping-cough. Within three months of her death, however, our desolate home was brightened by the birth of a second daughter, and then followed two other daughters, and, lastly, a son was given us.

After completing his education, he was articled to my brother-in-law, Mr. Bateson Wood, and has now become the head of the firm Wood & Williamson. I may say of him, and of myself, that from his birth until now he has given me no anxiety beyond what any little failure of health has caused, and some of the keenest pleasures possible to the heart of a father.

In 1854 my Wesleyan friends resolved to publish a quarterly journal of a higher literary and scientific character than any that had been previously attempted by them. They solicited my co-operation, which I promised to give, and wrote an article for their first number on " The Lower Forms of Vege-" table Life," the first of a long series which continued until 1869, when the pressure of other work compelled me to retire from their staff. The magazine was called the *London Quarterly*.

During this period I made two excursions with my friend, Mr. John Fernley, up the Rhine, and through Switzerland to the Italian Lakes. These visits familiarised me with Alpine flora, which I had previously known only from illustrated books; whilst they also gave me opportunities of indulging what had long been a favourite amusement—viz., landscape sketching in water colours.

Whilst events just recorded were passing, I was suddenly prostrated by illness. Operating upon a case of fistula, the point of my knife had slightly grazed the skin of my finger, and mortific matter had penetrated. Inflamed absorbents were followed by epilepsy, and my medical friends insisted upon my retiring from private practice for fifteen months, and abandoning my town residence for a more suburban one. Purchasing some land in the village of Fallowfield, a little more than three miles south of the Manchester Exchange, I had a house built and a large garden constructed. After returning to practice, I began to build hothouses, and gradually supplied myself with a number sufficient to cultivate all such plants as were required for my botanical classes. As time went on, garden and glasshouses gave me everything a professor of botany could need. Most of the rarer cryptogams, salvinias, marsileas, lycopodiaceous plants of almost every type grew most abundantly; orchids, saracenias, and four or five of the finest type of drosera flourished in profusion, and I reared dionæas from my own seed; thus ample provision was made for the supply of every want when the extension of botanical teaching, and especially the creation of the laboratory department, increased my requirements in the shape of specimens for dissection and microscopic study.

In the early summer of 1870, I took my family into Switzerland. In Paris I had several palæobotanical discussions with Professor Brongniart. From Paris we went to Strasburg, where I had arranged to spend some hours with Dr. Schimper. We then reached the Oberland by way of Schaffhausen and Zurich. At the latter place I should have met Prof. Heer, and only failed to do so through the blundering of a waiter at our hotel. We then went through the Oberland and over the Gemmi Pass to reach the Rhone, then crossed the Tête-Noir to Chamounix Valley, and returned home by way of Paris. Soon after our return, we celebrated the marriage of my eldest daughter.

During the early months of 1871 my dear wife suffered a martyrdom from some internal mischief. Towards midsummer the painful symptoms disappeared, only to return in still more serious form at the beginning of the following year. Within a limited number of days the inevitable blow fell upon our happy home circle.

Then came a long and dreary time of depression and sadness.

CHAPTER X

·OUR college quarters in Quay Street had long been too small for our needs, and, indeed, were so over-·crowded as to be more than inconvenient. Arrangements for erecting new buildings in Oxford Road were pushed, and the foundation-stone was laid by the late Duke of Devonshire on September 23, 1870.

This building was opened for regular work on ·October 7, 1873, and proved to be an enormous relief by affording space for doing our work, but it ·was still far from giving us all we wanted.

I had one room in which I was able to store my ·collection of objects used for the illustration of my lectures, which room I also utilised for a poor ·mockery of a laboratory.

Very shortly the amalgamation of the Royal School ·of Medicine and Surgery increased my number of

students and made it needful that I should have assistance. In 1878 Mr. Marcus Hartog was appointed
demonstrator, yet I was still Professor of Comparative
Anatomy, Zoology, and of Botany. The increasing
demands on the part of examining bodies for laboratory work, however, made this impossible, and in
the following year I resigned the Chair of Zoology
and Animal Physiology, that for the future I might
have time to fulfil the duties of my Botanical Chair
as they required to be performed in the then
advanced condition of botanical science.

In 1880 Professor Milnes Marshall was appointed
to the new Chair. For enthusiasm and energy,
backed by a profound knowledge of the fundamentals
of his subject, Milnes Marshall was one of the most
remarkable young men it was ever my lot to be
associated with. Unhappily, even as I am penning
these lines, we have to speak of him in the past
tense. He was unfortunately killed a few days ago
by falling down one of the precipitous slopes of
Scaw Fell.

Several years previously I had had in one of my
evening classes for botany a young man of the
name of Marshall Ward. I then lost sight of him
but subsequently found he had been pursuing a
brilliant course, partly at South Kensington, partly
at Cambridge, and lastly in Germany. He then
returned to Owens as my demonstrator and assistant
lecturer. After holding this office for a while he
accepted a Government commission to Ceylon,

to investigate the fungoid diseases that were
making such havoc amongst the coffee-plantations
of that island. On his return to Manchester, we
elected him to a Berkeley fellowship, then at our
disposal, in the department of botanical research.
Some time afterwards I was again in need of a
demonstrator; he resigned his fellowship, and once
more worked along with me. This he continued to
do until his own election to his present professorship at Cooper's Hill.* He soon was elected Fellow
of the Royal Society, and a few weeks ago I had the
rich pleasure of seeing him receive from the hands
of Lord Kelvin one of the Society's gold medals,
given in recognition of his most elaborate researches
in some of the obscure branches of vegetable physiology. Meanwhile, in addition to the changes already
recorded, I should mention some others of even greater
importance.

In 1880 the Queen granted us our charter, estab-
lishing the Victoria University, the seat of which
was to be permanently in Manchester. The three
teaching institutions ultimately united in this university were Owens College at Manchester, University College at Liverpool, and Yorkshire College
at Leeds. The two latter, however, became connected with us some time after the original granting
of the charter.

Meanwhile the charter fell short of all that was

* Professor Marshall Ward now holds the Chair of
Botany in Cambridge.—A. C. W.

wanted. Manchester had long possessed one, and more than once, *two* medical schools. But the first to be adequately equipped and established was that of Pine Street, founded by Mr. Thomas Turner.

In 1872 arrangements were agreed upon for uniting this, school with Owens College. In 1873 new buildings were begun in the college grounds for its reception. This school eventually became very successful, but the new University had no power officially to examine or to confer medical degrees upon its students. This was largely the result of opposition on the part of the Yorkshire College and the London College of Surgeons, the British Medical Association, and the heads of numerous medical schools both in London and in the provinces. In June 1882, a Royal Commission, appointed by Parliament to inquire into the working of the Medical Acts, recommended that the " power to grant its own medical degrees should be " given to the Victoria University." This recommendation settled the question. In April 1883 an additional charter authorised us to confer medical and surgical degrees upon our students.

In 1887 the magnificent new laboratories and lecture-rooms, erected parallel to Coupland Street for the departments of zoology, botany, and geology, were opened for work. Now, for the first time, the biological sciences had a chance of being taught in Owens College in an effective manner; and in August 1887 the new museum buildings, facing Oxford

Street, were so far completed as to be used by the British Association for the Advancement of Science for their Reception-rooms.

Soon afterwards the buildings were filled with cases for the reception of specimens. Here I obtained two good rooms in which to lay the foundation of a botanical museum. The fine herbarium of European plants, collected by the late H. C. Watson, had already been placed at my disposal by Sir Joseph Hooker, and is now preserved in the museum.

I have referred to the temporary cessation of my medical labours ; these, after being suspended fifteen months by illness, were actively resumed. Excepting some pamphlets in connection with my aural studies, I made no pretensions to becoming a medical author, but one class of cases did specially interest me. I had not unfrequently witnessed severe attacks of convulsions in infants only a few weeks old, and in 1855 I had charge of a very bad case of this kind in Stockport, near Manchester. The severity of the convulsions made me confident that the end must be almost immediate unless prompt relief was obtained. Judging that mischief was due to some internal irritant which the child's nervous system was unable to bear, I determined to try how far the inhalation of chloroform could be carried in the case of so young a child. Carefully attending to the necessary supply of air, I administered the chloroform on the folds of a fine cambric handkerchief, held at some distance

from the mouth. The convulsions gradually sub-
sided; in a few minutes I withdrew the chloroform,
but the convulsions quickly returned, and the chloroform was as immediately reapplied. The result was
that I kept the child continually under the influence
of the chloroform excepting partial relaxation of it
at intervals, to admit of the administration of a little
milk, drawn artificially from a wet nurse who was in
attendance. We continued this treatment from
December 19th to the 28th of the same month. The
result was a perfect success; the child had inhaled
twelve fluid ounces of chloroform.

Some years later I had a still more remarkable
case of the same kind, but on this occasion we had
to continue the operations for three weeks, the
child inhaling nineteen fluid ounces of chloroform. The method was as successful as before.
The conclusions at which I arrived, after treating a
number of similar cases in the same way were—
(1) that to be successful the use of the chloroform
must be continuous, not intermittent; (2) that no
artificial food should be given, but that a wet-nurse
should be employed from the commencement,
drawing the milk with a breast-pump and adminis-
tering it with a spoon. Whether this method has
been tried elsewhere, or whether newer fashions have
been proved better I do not know.

In 1876 I commenced another series of investigations, which are still in progress. Several of our
geological authors have called attention to two facts;

one, that some coals contain considerable numbers of spores, like the inflammable objects derived from recent lycopods, and long used in our theatres to produce artificial lightning. Another is that fragments of wood also are contained in some coals, the fibres or vessels of many of which are perforated by numerous rounded apertures. But nothing definite was known of the range, distribution, or nature of these objects. So having at this time a little more leisure than usual, I began a systematic study of the microscopic structure of coal, with the intention, if life was spared, of embracing the more important coals of the entire world; with this intention I obtained abundant supplies from various regions. Indeed, so many carefully packed consignments reached my house, that the railway carriers asked, " Do the " people here get all their coal in boxes"? and the room in which these researches were conducted was called my "coalhole." I made microscopic sections of nearly all our native kinds, and my cabinet already contains 361 of these sections, classified and arranged, besides a considerable number of miscellaneous ones made experimentally.

In like manner I made microscopic preparations of all the more important of the perforated tissues just referred to. Besides examining a large number of our British coals, I also studied those of New Zealand, Australia, South Africa, Japan, Borneo, Sweden, the Arctic regions, with some from India and Nova Scotia. I have been much disappointed that I have not been able to make more progress with this inquiry; but regarding the study of the organisation of the carboniferous plants as my more important task, coal has been set aside whenever the other became urgent. Still I don't despair of carrying the black investigation yet a little further.

The broad conclusions at which I have arrived are not unimportant. In the first place, coals vary enormously as to the amount of perforated tissues (mineral charcoal) that they contain. Those of South Wales and Belgium are almost undistinguishable from this point of view. In some of them half the substance of the coal consists of these fragments of mineral charcoal. Where such is the case, the spores, which are usually of two kinds, macrospores and microspores, are very scanty. Thus, in the Belgian coals that I have already examined, macrospores are absolutely non-existent, and microspores almost equally so. On the other hand, the perforated tissues are largely of two types, viz., those where the perforations are more or less circular, and those in which the apertures are what are known as " bordered pits."

The extraordinary fact is, that considering how many of the trees of the carboniferous forests were lepidodendroid and sigillarian, we should have expected that their contributions to the stock of mineral charcoal would have been conspicuous from its amount, but, on the contrary, the real scalariform vascular tissue which is the characteristic form seen in the woody axis of the above lycopodiaceous plants is conspicuous from its scarcity.

Of course the question is, what has become of these tissues? The spores, *i.e.*, seed-like bodies of the same plants, are there in vast quantities; but I have one most interesting specimen which indicates that the missing objects melted away into the brown structureless element which constitutes so large a part of the substance of coal. To the quadrate forms common amongst the fragments of mineral charcoal thus preserved, we find abundant parallels at the present day in old decaying tree stumps and in the blocks of wood burnt upon the home fires. If the latter examples be watched it will be noticed that in some kinds of woods the burning surface is broken up into small squares by deep cracks, the most conspicuous of which are transverse to the long axis of the burning block.

[Dr. Williamson sent specimens of the results of his researches in detachments to the museum of Owens College, Manchester. When his strength failed so seriously as to convince him that he would never complete his work, he asked his old friend and disciple, A. C. Seward, Esq., of St. John's College, Cambridge, to take possession of his notes and unworked material and continue the inquiry as circumstance permitted.—A. C. W.]

CHAPTER XI

IN the spring of 1873 I received an invitation from the Council of the British Association for the Advancement of Science to deliver the Friday evening lecture, and as the next meeting was arranged to be held at Bradford, the centre of the large coal-bearing district of Yorkshire, the council especially wished me to make my lecture embrace in some way the prevailing local industry. I had neither energy nor spirits for engaging in such an effort, and was therefore about to decline the invitation, but my children set their faces against my doing so. They urged that the council had paid me a great compliment in inviting me to deliver this lecture, and that the

L

prospect of, and the effort of preparing for it, would do much towards restoring my energies to their wonted level. Unable to resist their affectionate appeals, I undertook the task. Having consented, I resolved to do the work effectually, and so as to make it tributary to my campaign against the Brongniartian heresies which then prevailed throughout Europe and America. As the meeting of the Association approached, the public press became considerably confused about two names. The president of the meeting for that year was Alexander Williamson, the chemist, whilst I of course represented the biologists and geologists. We were queerly mixed in the newspapers, when *The Times* proceeded to set the public right, and succeeded only in increasing the confusion. All this led to fun when the President introduced me to the audience, and I mounted the rostrum at his summons. I had prepared for my work with the greatest care, and the lecture was pronounced a success. Before we left the platform Mr. Spottiswoode, who was present, asked me to deliver a course of afternoon lectures at the Royal Institution in Albemarle Street. This led at a subsequent date to my being invited by the late Sir William Bowman to deliver a second day course as well as one of the Friday evening lectures. About this time there sprang up throughout England and Scotland a demand for science lectures. This demand was promoted by the trustees of the Gilchrist Fund, on whose staff I was placed. The result was, that between the years 1874 and 1880 inclusive I delivered in sixty-one towns a hundred and fifty-eight lectures on various branches of the sciences that came within my range, and wholly apart from my lectures at the Owens College. My connection with the Gilchrist Trust continued until 1890, and during the latter ten years the number of lectures given was at least equal to that of the earlier ones.

During the Association Meeting at Bradford I was the guest of Mr. Henry, now Sir Henry Mitchell, and head of the Bradford branch of the large firm of A. and S. Henry & Co. On arriving at his house in Manningham I was received by Sir Henry's widowed sister, who for many years had super-intended his domestic establishment. My friend, Mr. Pengelly, and the popular Wesleyan preacher, Morley Puncheon, were fellow guests. Before the week ended I was casually introduced to a daughter of my hostess. During Easter week of the following year I again visited Sir Henry, and again met Miss Heaton, the result of which meeting was our engage-ment and marriage in the following year.

During the autumn of 1874 we were staying at the " Devonshire Arms," Bolton, in Wharfedale, when we found in the same hotel a gentleman already well known to me through his architectural writings, but whom I had never previously met. This was the Reverend Mackenzie Walcott, Precentor of Chichester Cathedral, and the eminent author of so

many widely known publications on the abbeys and
cathedrals of Great Britain. Our new acquaintance
and Mrs. Walcott accompanied us to the abbey, and
he gave us the benefit of his perfect knowledge of the
history and former outlines, as well as the characteristic peculiarities which distinguished Bolton
Abbey from other similar relics of bygone ages.
During our stroll he discovered that I was a
botanist, and immediately proposed a bargain. I
was to give him botanical instruction based upon
the plants and flowers still abundant in the
higher parts of the Yorkshire dales, and he would
instruct me in the leading features of ancient
ecclesiastical ruins. This plan was most pleasantly
carried out during the remainder of our stay in
Bolton, and our friendship continued until Mr.
Walcott's death, some years later. Leaving Bolton,
we drove over the hills into Airedale, as far as
Settle, staying a day at Malham. At Settle I was
anxious to visit the recently discovered Victoria
Cave, and hearing that Mr. Tiddeman, the Government geologist, in whose hands the exploration of
the cave was placed, had already gone to it, we
hurried after him, to secure, if possible, the benefit
of his intelligent guidance in examining it. When
nearly a mile from the spot we met him returning ;
but on seeing us, he most kindly retraced his
steps and took us along with him. This cavern
is an unusually interesting one. A large portion of
its floor was occupied, when first explored, with

three distinct superimposed layers of earth, each one representing a defunct and prolonged period of the history of the cave since its formation. The uppermost layer contained numerous bones of the wild boar, badger, fox, bear, and reindeer—evidently animals belonging to one of the later epochs of the world's geological history. The presence of the reindeer suggests a time not much later than the glacial period. Then came a bed, some ten or twelve feet thick, which contains no remains of animal life whatever. The third and lowest layer seems to be the thickest of the series, and in it were bones of the primeval elephant, rhinoceros, hippopotamus, bear, bison, and hyæna. It thus appears most probable that the lowest of these three deposits was formed when the cave was the home of the hyæna, fragments of the other and larger animals being carried in piecemeal, apparently during an epoch preceding that in which Europe was what Greenland now is, covered with a vast ice sheet. In like manner the uppermost layer of rubbish had accumulated when most of the older animals had become extinct in Britain, and the ice sheet had disappeared. The cave was then a den of bears, which animals still survive in Europe, from which the hyæna disappeared long ago.

After several pleasant visits, we journeyed to Keswick, where my children and one of Sir Henry Mitchell's sons were awaiting us. Here again we made pleasant acquaintances; lodging in the next house to that in which we were living, was a gentleman, evidently a clergyman who took my fancy. On making inquiries, I found he was the Reverend John Charles Ryle, the well-known writer of religious tracts, and now the Bishop of Liverpool. I had long been familiar both with his name and his works; I now found an intelligent and enthusiastic field geologist. Canon Ryle had exchanged clerical duties for a season with the clergyman of the parish church at Keswick, but his weekdays were largely devoted to long pedestrian rambles, in search of some of the more interesting phenomena with which this old hunting ground of Adam Sedgwick so largely abounded. He thought nothing of walking twenty miles to see some junction of igneous rocks with the stratified slates of the district : and altogether I had discovered a delightful companion.

Whilst staying at Keswick, I had the pleasure of making two water-colour sketches of Thirlmere from its eastern end, views of the lovely lake that can never again be seen by travellers. Mr. Stanley Leathes kindly lent us his boat to enable us to hunt out the best points of view. After our day's picnic we returned to Mr. Leathes to deliver the key of his boathouse and found ourselves, travel-stained as we were, in the midst of a large and brilliant garden-party, from which our host's kindness would allow of no escape.

The next autumn, after the birth of our son Herbert Crawford, the whole family adjourned again to Bolton in Wharfedale ; this time, however, we lived in a farmhouse. During our stay we had large opportunity of experiencing the genial and gracious kindness of the late Duke of Devonshire. The Duke and his party were staying at the Abbey for shooting, consequently all surrounding tenants were requisitioned by the steward to supply poultry, eggs, butter, trout, in fact everything; and as we were seven miles from any shop, our table might have been uncomfortable, but the Duke, knowing we were in the neighbourhood, gave orders that some addition of game, poultry, or fish should be sent to us every day.

One day the Duke happened to show me a small wound on the front of the shin-bone. Every experienced surgeon knows that few accidents are more likely, if neglected, to cause trouble than this. The Duke's sore was beginning to look fiery and threatening, but by persuading my patient to rest for a few days, and applying the tepid water-dressing, the value of which I had learnt in my hospital days from its great master, Liston, an improvement quickly took place.

One sad incident marred the pleasure of this holiday. My second daughter, Minnie, had for some time past been far from well, and it now began to be apparent that mischief more serious and more deeply organic than I had hitherto supposed was the cause. The subsequent year showed that we had but too much reason for our anxieties.

The meeting of the British Association was this year held in Bristol. Leaving my people in their farmhouse home, I went down for a few days, and stayed at the house of Mr. Fry, the celebrated chocolate manufacturer. My fellow guest was Dr. Farr, Superintendent of the Statistical Department of the General Register's Office. Fun and merriment were not absent from the little circle. Among other amusing facts narrated by Dr. Farr was the somewhat startling one, that after the age of forty-five years, eleven widows married to one maiden lady.

During this visit I had an example of the erroneous judgments arrived at from mere external appearances. At a large breakfast-party where our host was a member of the Bristol Corporation, I found myself seated by the side of a gentleman, who was a stranger to me. The scientific circle was brilliant, but my neighbour never opened his lips so long as we sat side by side. I tried to imagine who he was, and concluded he was some one very much out of his sphere, and very uncomfortable, with no interest in the flow of conversation around him. Judge of my astonishment when I discovered my silent neighbour was no other than James Joseph Sylvester, and that I, in my undiscerning stupidity, had spent a silent hour side by side with one of the very foremost mathematicians in the world.

In 1876 the British Association held its meeting in Glasgow, where my wife and I were the guests of Mr. J. Napier, the active partner of the eminent

firm of shipbuilders of that name. One of the most
interesting events of the meeting to me was an
expedition to the Island of Arran. My new friend
Mr. Wunsch was on board the boat, he had recently
made the discovery of a carboniferous forest that
had become buried in volcanic ash at Laggan Bay,
near the fallen rocks on the eastern shore of the
island. The stumps of several huge lepidodendra
remained in their original positions, and the steamer
lay to opposite the forest, whilst Mr. Wunsch and I,
along with a few strangers, went on shore in a boat
to bring on board one of the finest of these stumps,
which had been dug out in readiness for us, a few
days previously. In the meantime Archibald Geikie,
the head of the Scottish Geological Survey, had
intimated to me that it would be acceptable to the
guests on deck if I would mount to the bridge of
the steamer and give them a short address on the
subject of carboniferous flora, including that of
Laggan Bay, which I did. Afterwards, as I was
explaining the peculiar features of this tree to the
President of the Association and some of his family
who were on the steamer, I was interrupted by a
violent oratorical attack from a strange, clerical
looking Scotchman, who denounced me, not only for
what I had just been saying to the President, but
also for my little lecture from the bridge. He
said I was preaching a doctrine of devils, I
presume by referring to the great antiquity
of my plants, that I was misleading souls and

sending them to a place that shall be nameless now, though he named it clearly enough then. I tried to rid myself of the rude fellow, but failed, until I called upon the President to exercise his official authority, and silence him. Mr. Wunsch ascertained who this champion of orthodoxy was, and happening on the succeeding Sunday to be in the neighbour-hood of the Presbyterian chapel in which my assailant habitually held forth, he went in, and, oddly enough, found the preacher expounding to his people what had taken place, and with what a " Doctrine of Devils " I had sought to lead the souls of pious Scotchmen away from the truth.

It was evidently fortunate for me the days of the Inquisition were passed. One of the most crowded of the meetings this year was in the geological sec-tion, where the Duke of Argyll was announced to read a paper on the subject of the glacial epoch, to the existence of which he was always opposed. He knew, wisely enough, that the case of Greenland afforded a strong argument in support of the glacialists; but he disputed the accuracy of their interpretation of the conditions of that country. Our view has always been that it was a huge continent covered by a sheet of ice of unknown thickness. He denied that this was the case, and argued that the country consisted of a low group of islands, separated by narrow channels, upon which a merely thin layer of ice and snow rested. Naturally, my reply was that the huge glaciers flowing

from the ice-sheet were much too gigantic to be dis-
charged from such a country as he supposed Greenland to be, especially that such a phenomenon as
the Humboldt glacier, fifty miles across from side to
side, was an impossibility under his conditions.
It is needless to ask, after Dr. Nansen's gallant
explorations, which of us was right.

In the summer of 1877 we fixed our holiday
quarters at Dunoon, in order to be within reach of
Laggan Bay, which I was anxious to submit to a
further examination. Having arranged with my
friend, Mr. Wunsch, to meet us there, and having
ascertained that, if we would be content with such
sleeping quarters as a shepherd's hut could afford,
we not only could stay all night, but should be
heartily welcomed, my wife and I found our way
there as best we could. On reaching Corrie, our
first business was to secure a boat and boatmen to
take us to Laggan Bay; but this was no easy task,
as most of the many boats we saw were private
property, and most of the fine manly race of fellows
were fishermen. At last we met a miserable-looking
creature, who for an exorbitant fee consented to row
us; and, utterly unable to find anything better, we
accepted his services. It took us nearly an hour to
reach the stream that comes down from Glen Sannox.
Another fifteen minutes was lost through the unfortunate discovery that a beautiful young seal was
reposing on some rocks a little to the north of the
Sannox stream. This seal our boatman insisted upon

catching—an exploit which he failed to achieve. Much to our delight, just as we came within a few yards of it, and our man was making his preparations for knocking the innocent little creature on the head, it slipped from the rock, went under our boat into deep water, and did not reappear until it was beyond the reach of danger. I almost thought I saw the little animal give its would-be capturer something uncommonly like a wink of derision as it escaped his hands. After this, it became obvious the man was wholly unequal to the task he had undertaken; so we compelled him to put us on shore, and we walked the rest of the way to our destination. Soon after our arrival, we saw Mr. Wunsch descending a mountain path to meet us, he having come by way of Loch Ranza; and we were soon at work exploring our fossil forest.

Quite near our forest was a narrow strip of flat ground running parallel with the shore, but a few yards above the reach of the tides. Part of this was converted into a small field of barley; the remainder was a pleasant bit of greensward, on which roamed a number of varied farmyard inhabitants, whilst in the centre was planted our tiny shepherd's hut, apparently the only building with a roof on it within many miles. Behind the house arose rapidly the fine range of hills running northwards towards Loch Ranza and westward into the centre of the island. After an hour or two of hard work, hunger drove us to look after our lodgings and food. We found a minute, one-storeyed house, with a door in the middle, a window on each side of it, a deep thatched roof, and a shed built on the left side. Looking in at the door, we found a large square room, evidently the "house"; on the hearth-stone glowed a fire of brilliant peat ash. Opposite us were two beds in the wall, made after the fashion of ship berths; somewhere a loud clock ticked; there were a few chairs, a couple of tables, a lot of children, and a good, kindly housewife, who greeted us right warmly, and said, our "tea would be ready "in a few minutes." Meanwhile, "would the lady "like to see her bedroom?" and she showed us a door, on the left wall of the house, which led into a minute apartment, perhaps the smallest I ever slept in. Behind this closet was a large room stocked with skins, and on another side of it a cowhouse containing cow and calf, who serenaded us all night. Our little room contained two glorious carved oak chests, a single chair, a small oak bedstead, solid and box-like, a very large number of sheep and calf skins, which were crammed under the bed and into every corner of the place; and upon a deep, lovely window-seat rested a family Bible, Burns's Poems, the "Pilgrim's Progress," and a Scottish Psalmody. Our hearts sank a little at the thought of the skins, and what live-stock they might contain; but we were in for a spree, and this was part of the fun. Mr. Wunsch was to sleep in one of the berths in the "house"; the shepherd, his wife, his wife's sister,.

and all the children, we presume, slept in the other
—at least we heard nothing to the contrary.

When we had investigated for a few minutes, our
hostess called us for tea; and there on the greensward we found a table laden with cakes freshly
baked in peat ash, piles of fresh butter, and tea such
as I had never dreamed of before.   We three sat at
the table; around us were fowls, ducks, geese, pigs in
plenty, dogs, cats, donkeys, and children, all somewhat
astonished at the innovation.   We had the mountains
behind us, the sea in front; beyond, the Ayrshire
coast, the mouth of the Clyde, and the Island of
Bute; whilst to the north stretched the placid waters
of Loch Fyne, alive with herring-boats.   A few
yards from us gurgled a lovely little mountain
stream—our only lavatory.

We spent the evening climbing the mountains,
watching the setting sun, and revelling in the purity
of the air and beauty of the situation.

As may be imagined, we retired late and rose
early; but were scarcely ready when we saw a boat
approaching, rowed by a couple of vigorous quarrymen, who not only brought us fine fresh fish and
bread for breakfast, but were come to help us in
digging out our trees.   Breakfast was, if possible, an
improvement even upon our tea of the previous day,
insomuch as now everything glistened in morning
light and sparkled with dew.   After a hearty meal,
we set to work, first clearing away much of a hard
layer of volcanic ash under which the cluster of

trees was buried, and thus exposing additional stems.
These were generally about two feet in diameter, and
mostly in a curious condition. They were merely
cylinders of the outer barks, all the more internal
structures had disappeared. In addition to the more
delicate internal zones of the bark, each trunk should
have had a strong central axis of pith and woody
tissue, nearly three inches in diameter, but of this
no trace remained. Fragments of these axes were
discernible here and there in the surrounding volcanic ash, but none in the trees themselves. However, one large stem contained no fewer than six of
these missing structures, most of them being of the
largest size ; whilst associated with them, within the
cortical cylinder, was a large quantity of foreign
vegetable material, including fragments of the roots
of these trees, now known as Stigmaria. It was
impossible that more than one of these vascular axes
could have belonged to the tree in which we discovered them. What had happened is not difficult to sur-
mise. There had primarily been a grove of trees growing on the spot where we found their remains. When
living, they were in the centre of a region as volcanic
as Auvergne. Nevertheless, the trees continued to
flourish until they attained to their maximum
normal dimensions, but at length they perished,
probably in consequence of the mephitic vapours
which filled the atmosphere, and were derived not
only from the volcanic vents with which Arran itself
must have abounded, but also from the volcanoes of

Ayrshire. Anyhow, they were killed, and as time rolled on their upper stems and branches perished and disappeared, nothing remaining but their dwarf stumps, such as are common where what are called submarine forests exist.

Wherever we discover such trees preserved in a fossil state we find that the inner layers of the bark are the first to disappear, the outer cortex being composed of a strong fibrous material, which resists destructive agencies. But it was these inner layers of the bark that held the central vascular axis in its place. At the same period the trees must have become submerged, when the water which overflowed them would float out all the loose decaying vegetable matter which the protective bark on each trunk would otherwise have retained within its cylindrical walls. The state of all our stems excepting one shows, that not only the fragments of the inner cortex were thus removed, but that each central vascular axis floated out along with them. Hence it is that we found the interiors of most of these trees filled with pure volcanic ash, almost unmixed with any vegetable elements. But something more had happened to one exceptional tree, a large transverse section of which is now in the entrance of my house, whilst the remainder I presented to Owens College, and it is now one of the treasures of the geological museum.

This tree must have passed through the same stages of decay, and the disappearance of its inner tissues, as its companions. It had been converted into a hollow vertical receptacle submerged by the tide, which had in like manner emptied the other stems of their contents. But it is evident that the material and several branches and rootlets thus floated out had not gone very far away. Some fortunate current brought them back to the spot on which our one tree stood and poured them into its hollow cavity, where some shower of volcanic ash permanently plugged them, and where they remained until the time of our visit.

The tree thus preserved is more instructive than any other that has come under my notice from any part of the world.

CHAPTER XII

The Union of Yorkshire Naturalists—Lecture at Malton—
Agricultural controversy—Fossil Fucoids—Memoir on
undescribed tracks of invertebrate animals from the
Yoredale rocks—Imitative water marks—Sigillaria and
Stigmaria—Monograph for the Palæontographical Society—The Clayton fossil tree—Positions of responsibility and distinction—Meeting of British Association
in Manchester.

THE Yorkshire Union of Naturalists, of which I
first became an honorary member and subsequently
president, is one of the most influential and energetic
of the many scientific institutions that exist in
the country. Its centre and the residence of
its official secretaries is at Leeds, but it has an
immense number of local centres or branch institutions diffused throughout the country, at one or
another of which its annual meetings are held. It
is therefore largely a peripatetic society, but its more
energetic supporters were to be found in the districts
round Leeds, Bradford, and Halifax.

During the summer a succession of excursions is
made to the more scientifically interesting localities

in the neighbourhood, and as these visits not in-
frequently bring the members into districts where
no branch has hitherto been organised, the stimulus
given by the gathering very frequently leads to one
being formed. On one of these occasions, whilst I
was in the presidential chair, we took the excursionists
to Malton, where there was as yet no Society, but
being among friends, and as there was in the town
a small museum sustained by a few active naturalists,
I had no difficulty in persuading the Maltonians to
establish such a branch. They only consented to do
so on condition that I would become its president,
which I promised to do. This of course involved
my running over to Malton from time to time, to give
the young Society an address on some scientific
subject.

On one of these occasions, being in the midst of
an agricultural district, I selected for my subject the
manuring of the land. Brought up in the midst of
the Yorkshire farmers near my native town, I had
long been convinced that their land was inadequately
manured, and some of the German botanical writers
on plant feeding had given me further scientific light
on the subject. They demonstrated that the larger
the amount of manure the soil contained, the more
the plants took up. There might already be present
more than the plants absolutely needed, if they
absorbed all there was within their reach ; but this
was precisely what they did not do, consequently
they were benefited by a superabundance. On one

occasion I travelled through the highly cultivated
Lothians with an intelligent gentleman farmer, from
whom I naturally sought all the information I could
obtain respecting the secrets of their success, and
after calling my attention to the low, well-clipped
fences and almost entire absence of ditches, he turned
to the subject of manure. He informed me that his
farm was but of moderate size, its stock furnished
him with a fair supply of manure, the whole of which
was put into the ground; nevertheless he had that
spring expended fifty pounds in the purchase of
additional manure, the whole of which had also
been put into the soil. I asked him how far the
crops would repay that large investment notwithstanding all the advantages of their six-course
system. He replied that he had no fears whatever
on that point. Having these facts clear in my mind,
I gave my lecture at Malton, which at once raised a
storm. The country newspapers assailed me right
and left. Letters from farmers told me what nonsense
I had been talking; that although I did not know it,
any manure left in the ground in autumn would be
washed out of it by the rains of winter. To my
surprise, even the *Leeds Mercury* took up this absurd
cuckoo cry. Of the smaller fry of my assailants I took
no notice whatever, but I replied to a second comment
upon my teaching in the *Mercury*. I invited the writer
to visit my garden near Manchester, where we
certainly had rain enough, but where I could show
him hollyhocks and hungry sunflowers from five to

seven feet high, growing in borders which, well manured five years previously, had not subsequently received a single ounce. I begged him therefore to tell me whence these plants got their needful nitrogen. Whilst this storm was blowing, I asked my oldest living friend and schoolfellow, Professor Gilbert, the distinguished colleague of Sir John Lawes, how long a soil thus well manured would retain traces of it. He replied " For fifteen years." This knocked on the head the washing-out theory of the farmers. The address certainly made a sensation, and I received an application for a copy of it from the editor of the leading agricultural newspaper in the northern half of Scotland, who republished it *verbatim*. A similar application reached me from the south of the Thames.

Between the years 1823 and 1881 a copious literature was produced on a subject of considerable scientific interest. Certain peculiar objects had been found in the strata of various ages, respecting which great differences of opinion existed. My friend, Dr. Nathorst, of Stockholm, published a memoir in 1881, in which he supplied a bibliography containing no fewer than 130 writers who had written on the above objects during the previous sixty years.

The question at issue was the real nature of the fossilised specimens just referred to. The greater number of the above writers regarded them as fossil Fucoids.

This was especially the case with another of my

old friends, Professor Schimper of Strasburg, who introduced into his well-known " Paléontologie Végétale " a large number of genera and species of these questionable objects.

Schimper's example has still more recently been followed by the Marquis de Saporta of Aix. The determinations of the latter author have been vigorously controverted by Professor Nathorst, who tried a number of very important experiments resembling those made by Professor Buckland many years ago, when the reptilian footsteps of Corn-Cockle-Muir were first discovered and their nature much debated. Professor Nathorst made various aquatic animals travel under water, leaving behind them, as they did so, very definite tracks on fine mud, and he published photographs of these tracks, so that no artistic errors could creep into his figures of them.

In 1885 I received from the Rev. Isidore Kavannah, of Montreal, then a student of the Roman Catholic College of Stonyhurst, in Lancashire, some interesting specimens which he had discovered upon loose blocks of stone strewing the shore of the Ribble, close to the college. The bank of the stream at this point is composed of what are known geologically as Yoredale rocks, a series of beds that intervene between the millstone grit and the mountain limestone.

The controversy between my two friends, Saporta and Nathorst, illustrated as it was by the beautiful objects obtained from Stonyhurst, led me to give special attention to these anomalous organisms, and my results were embodied in a memoir, "On "some Undescribed Tracks of Invertebrate Animals "from the Yoredale Rocks, and on some Inorganic "Phenomena Produced on Tidal Shores, Simulating "Plant Remains." This memoir was published in the tenth volume of the third series of "Memoirs of the "Manchester Literary and Philosophical Society," session 1884–1885.

During a holiday at Llanfairfechan, in North Wales, two years prior to the above date, my attention was arrested by the small drainage streams that followed the retiring tide. I cannot better explain the nature of these conditions than by quoting a brief passage or two from my memoir. "These contours, produced by many of the smaller "tributaries, where they united to form larger "streamlets, suggested to my mind the extreme "probability that the casts of such sculptured areas "would, if found in any of the older strata, be un- "distinguishable from many of the so-called fossil "Fucoids found in these strata." I succeeded in obtaining a number of plaster casts of the more striking of these conditions, and presented them to Owens College Museum, where they are now pre- served, and photographs of some of these casts illustrate my memoir. Had such specimens been found on the inferior surfaces of ancient flag- stones, I have little doubt but that they would have appeared in the pages of Schimper and other authors with similar views, as Palæozoic Fucoid forms of plant life.

On visiting Barmouth at a later date, I was naturally on the look-out for similar pseudophytes. "Products of tidal action and drainage were not "wanting, but to my surprise, those of the new "locality were wholly different from what I found "on the Carnarvonshire coast." Yet, though different, they were not the less plant-like. The shore was covered with tidal ripple marks, which were cut through obliquely by drainage streamlets. Casts were made, as before, of these new forms, and photographs of them published in my memoir. They resemble the overlapping scale leaves of some cycadean stems, and probably might have been mistaken for such, had they been discovered on some slab of oolitic sandstone.

Still another important palæo-botanical question had agitated scientific thinkers for many years past, without reaching a satisfactory solution. One of the most abundant of the fossil plants found in the carboniferous rocks was that to which Brongniart originally gave the name of Stigmaria ficoides. The wildest notions were prevalent up to a late period respecting this object. It was believed to be a huge floating aquatic plant, in which long, sub-dividing branches radiated from a central dome-shaped axis, the branches being furnished with leaves arranged in an approach to a quincuncial geometric pattern. But an important discovery was

made in 1837, which threw a wholly new light upon
these objects. When the late Sir John Hawkshaw
was constructing the railway between Manchester
and Bolton, the workmen cut through a small group
of the bases of some gigantic Sigillarian trees. Casts
of two of these trees are now preserved in the
Museum of the Owens College of Manchester, and
figures of them are given in Plate I. of my monograph on the " Morphology and Histology of Stigmaria ficoides," published in 1887. Four huge primary
roots branched off from these trees, which were
soon afterwards identified by my old friends, Mr.
Binney and Mr. John Eddowes Bowman, as being
true examples of the well-known Stigmaria, and
which they at once pronounced to be the roots of
Sigillariæ. Other similar specimens were discovered
in various parts of Lancashire, but, unfortunately,
none of these are capable of being preserved in a
museum, nor could the actual continuity of the roots
with the central stem be demonstrated; hence, in
many quarters doubt continued to be expressed
respecting the accuracy of the observations of the
Manchester geologists.

This was the position of the question when I
proposed to the Palæontographical Society the
publication of my monograph on Stigmaria ficoides.
This offer was accepted, and in 1886 my manuscript
and figures were handed over to the Society. It is,
I believe, unquestioned that I had in my cabinet at
that time the finest collection in the world of micro-

scopic sections and other specimens illustrating the history of this plant, but we were still in the unsatisfactory condition bequeathed to us by Mr. Binney, of the absence of museum specimens demonstrating the continuity of the roots with the stem.

The greater part of my memoir was already printed when I received a note from the late Mr. J. Davis of Chevin Edge, Halifax, announcing the discovery of a grand tree with Stigmarian roots at the village of Clayton, near Bradford, in Yorkshire. I at once hastened to the spot, and found the huge specimen resting upon a platform of carboniferous sandstone, and with the exception of the tips of some of its longest roots laid beautifully bare by the quarrymen.*

* On the morning we had arranged to see the Clayton tree, rain poured in torrents, and I tried in vain to persuade Dr. Williamson to postpone his journey. At Halifax we left the main line for a local one, after travelling several miles up hill; we went out into the rain, and proceeded to tramp along unprotected upland paths, or in sodden grass, through a perfect hurricane of howling wind; before half the distance was accomplished, our boots had become pools, and our clothes were saturated.

When we reached the quarry not a living soul was near, only the grey sky above, grey Yorkshire hills around, and the storm raging, when the old geologist met face to face the thing he had hoped so long to see. As he stood and gazed at the calm big tree spreading its roots in every direction, and apparently as full of life as it had ever been, the quarry

Assisted by the generosity of my eldest son and a few friends, I at once negotiated the purchase of the specimen as it stood, the removal to be accomplished at my expense. This was a work of time and patience, but the tree was at last presented to the Owens College Museum, and now stands without a rival for magnitude and grandeur in any of the museums of the world.

This specimen luckily came into my possession in time for a photograph and measurements of it to be included in my monograph. Other examples of the same kind, though much smaller, have been discovered, and one of which is preserved.

During the years in which I had been engaged in the inquiries described, I had filled various Presidential chairs. For more than twenty years I occupied that position in the large Manchester Society of Scientific Students. In 1882 I became President of the Microscopic and Natural History section of the Manchester Philosophical and Literary Society. In 1880–1882, I was President of the large Union of Yorkshire Naturalists. I presided over the Geological Section of the British Association for the Advancement of Science at its meeting in Southport, September 1884; the same year

master appeared, looking astonished, and said, "Not Profes-" sor Williamson !" "Certainly." "And from Manchester" this morning," said the shivering owner. "Yes, and why" not ?" "Well, sir," answered he, "to my thinking, you" and the tree are a pair, for teaching us lessons."

I became President of the Literary and Philosophical Society of Manchester. In 1889 the Geological Society of London did me the honour of awarding me the Wollaston Gold Medal. The University of Göttingen, the Royal Society of Stockholm, and the Natural History Society of Geneva elected me honorary member. The Geological, Microscopic, and Quekett Societies of London did me the same honour. Indeed, I had no reason to complain of neglect or forgetfulness on the part of my scientific brethren.

The British Association for the Advancement of Science arranged to hold its meeting of 1887 in Manchester, and a few of us determined to spare no efforts to make the meeting a success. I was especially anxious to bring to it a brilliant gathering of botanists, and began my efforts to do so early in the spring, by writing to Dr. and Mrs. Asa Gray of Harvard. I was disappointed on receiving a reply intimating that they would not be able to come, but I sent a second letter by return post, saying they *must* come ; we wanted them to be our personal guests, and could not dispense with them. Dr. Gray replied that as they were so evidently needed, they had not only decided to come, but had taken berths in an early steamer, in order to secure time for a Continental trip. So far, well. I then appealed to Professor de Barie of Strasburg, the Marquis de Saporta of Aix, Prof. Cohn of Breslau, Prof. Sachs of Würzburg, Professor

Graf zu Solmes Laubach [then] of Berlin, and finding that Professor Treub of the Botanic Gardens in Java was coming to England, I wrote to him. All these friends responded to my call excepting Sachs, who was too much of an invalid to leave home. Dr. and Mrs. Asa Gray, Professor de Barie, the Marquis de Saporta and his son, stayed in my own house. I had written as I thought to Professor Pringsheim of Berlin; he promised to come, and I secured for him a pleasant home with one of my friends; he arrived a day or two before the meeting commenced, when I received a note from his host, saying: "You told me Professor Pringsheim "was a botanist, but he is a chemist." I saw at once there was some mistake, and on inquiry discovered there were two professors of the same name in Berlin. I instantly telegraphed to the botanist, who came at once—hence my accident brought two distinguished men instead of one, for the chemist proved to be an excellent addition to our gathering. I happened to be one of the vice-presidents of my section, and having so unwonted a gathering of distinguished botanists under my chairmanship, we held our meetings apart from the zoologists, who were strong enough to dispense with our help.

We hoped to bring around our own table as many of the assembled naturalists as possible, but found we needed guidance in arranging foreign guests. In order to avoid *contretemps*, our good friend Graf zu Solmes Laubach, who knew most of the assembled

Germans, came each morning to overhaul my wife's invitation list ; to his kind help we are indebted for pleasant intercourse with our many guests. We had found that at other meetings the Sunday afternoons were often dull, and tried to prevent this for our friends, by issuing invitations for a small assembly of naturalists in our own house and garden. Fortunately the afternoon was fine. I believe every invited guest arrived, and many of our intimate neighbours who were not invited. We were glad our little effort was so kindly responded to. One enthusiastic friend said to my wife that "most of "the distinguished botanists of Europe and America "were in the garden, and not one but who had seen "something growing he never saw before."

CHAPTER XIII

Vegetable remains in the carboniferous rocks—Sternbergia approximata—M. Brongniart's " Prodrome d'une Histoire des Végétaux Fossiles "—Mr. Dawes of Birmingham—My first sections of Calamites—Mr. Binney's investigations—M. Grand' Eury—My first memoir—M. Brongniart's " Histoire des Végétaux Fossiles "—Cryptogamic nature of the most ancient fossil plants—Exogenous growth in Calamites and Sigillaria—Declared by M. Brongniart not to be Cryptogams—Mr. Butterworth of Oldham—Second memoir—Series of memoirs for the Royal Society " On the Organisation of the Fossil " Plants of the Coal Measures "—British Association at Edinburgh—Controversy in *Nature*—Views of M. Renault, M. Grand' Eury, and the Marquis de Saporta —Memoir for the *Annales des Sciences Naturelles*— M. Grand' Eury accepts view that Calamites and Sigillaria are Cryptogams.

GEOLOGISTS had long been familiar with some remarkable vegetable remains obtained from the carboniferous rocks. These were first figured very imperfectly by Sternberg, and again, in 1825, by Artis, under the name of Sternbergia approximata. In 1828 Brongniart noticed these curious fossils in his "Prodrome d'une Histoire des Végétaux Fossiles," and only referred them to some doubtful family of monocotyledons. In 1846, Mr. Dawes of Birmingham made a much closer approximation to the truth when he suggested that they were more probably the piths of some arborescent plant like Lepidodendron. In his " Tableaux des Genres des Végétaux Fossiles," published in 1849, Brongniart still inclined to his monocotyledonous suggestions, but at the date in question no definite conclusions had been arrived at. About this time I obtained some fine specimens of these objects, especially a young twig, in a good state of preservation, from the coal-field of Coalbrookdale, for which I was indebted to my friend, now Professor Prestwich.

Combining my microscopic preparations of this plant with others in my cabinet, I succeeded in discovering the interpretation of their structure. I should say that what looked like a pith resembled a vertical column of coins like pennies, but in most cases thicker and with very prominent round edges. So far as he went, Dawes was right in his suggestion that Sternbergia resembled a cast of a pith, but none of the observers who had studied these objects seem to have been familiar with any living plant in which a similar pith exists.

It soon struck me that it had been of the form known to the later botanists by the name of "discoid." In this type the periphery of the medulla is a continuous thin layer of cellular cylinder; but its more central portion splits up horizontally into

numerous thin transverse separable layers. Medullæ
of this type are found in the white jasmine, in the
common walnut, and some others of the Juglandaceæ,
and in the balsam pine of Canada. The wood and
bark of my specimens were of the common quasi-
coniferous form so frequently met with in the carboniferous rocks, then known by the name of
Dadoxylon, and now regarded as being of a gymnospermous type, half coniferous and half cycadean.
This successful investigation brought me back in
thought to my old subject of fossil botany, and
two casual incidents led the way to my devoting my
leisure hours to palæo-botanical subjects during the
remainder of my life.

Early in the fifties, when I was commencing in
an unsystematic way to grind down fragments of
various objects for microscopic investigation, I found
in a drawer of my cabinet a portion of a Calamite
that had been extracted from one of the ironstone
nodules of the coal-measures. I was not at that
time provided with a lathe or any other sort of
cutting or grinding machinery; but as the calamite
presented indications that some structure might
be found in it, I chipped off with hammer and chisel
such fragments as appeared suitable, and ground
them down on a flagstone, obtaining nine curious
sections, showing the structure of a woody zone
where it was in immediate contact with the
medulla.

Having then no intention of making any special

use of these preparations, they were put away in a drawer of the cabinet and almost forgotten.

About the same time I had instructed a working joiner to fit up for me a small horizontal grinding-wheel, worked by a pedal, and which was now complete. Somehow this little transaction gave the joiner the idea that I was interested in stones; and one evening he called upon me, bringing in his apron a number of rough fragments of sandstone. He had been working at a stone quarry near Oldham, and had picked up from the refuse of the quarry a basketful of stones which appeared new to him, and he concluded that they might be interesting to me. They were in the main the merest rubbish, but amongst them I detected a fragment which was equally elegant and remarkable. How it had escaped destruction from the unprotected way in which it had travelled in such rough company was to me an absolute mystery. The specimen looked like the base of one Calamite within the interior of a single joint of another and much larger one; but at that time I was wholly unable to construct any reasonable hypothesis explaining how the two parts had been brought into mutual relationship.

In later days, when the specimen so oddly and accidentally obtained, came to be intelligently studied, its history became clear enough, and the priceless fragment is now one of the most precious gems in my cabinet. Some time after the occurrence of the above event Sir Charles Lyell happened to be at my house, and I showed him this specimen. He was much struck with its interest and novelty, and asked me to allow him to publish a figure of it in the fifth edition of his "Manual of Elementary Geology," upon the preparation of which he was then engaged. Of course I consented, and the figure appeared in 1855 on page 368 of that work, whilst on page 372 of the same volume its author illustrated my recent discovery of the true structure of the Sternbergia, already referred to, by copying some of my figures.

At this time I had no intention of entering upon the long series of studies of the carboniferous plants in which I subsequently became engaged. My friend Mr. Binney was then investigating these plants, and I had no desire to interfere with his researches, but unfortunately he was not a botanist, and so fell into serious mistakes.

Soon after the publication of Lyell's volume just spoken of, I received a letter from M. Grand' Eury, of St. Etienne, in France, who, I afterwards learnt, was a rising colliery engineer in that part of the world.

In his letter he asked me some questions about the specimen of Calamite figured by Lyell, adding further remarks, obviously intended to elicit an expression of my views respecting the organisation of Calamites in general. To be honest, I must confess that I had then entirely forgotten the little I ever knew about that subject. To refresh my memory before replying to my correspondent, I hunted for and, with some difficulty, found my nine sections mentioned on a previous page. On studying them, and comparing them with Mr. Binney's figures and the descriptions of his Calamites, I soon found that the two did not agree. M. Grand' Eury became, and up to the present day continues to be, one of my most valued foreign correspondents. Further references to his work will follow presently.

The discrepancies between Mr. Binney's descriptions of Calamites and my sections led me to devote some time to a careful study of the question. It soon became clear to me that his specimens and mine belonged to two distinct modifications of the Calamitean type. Hence I resolved to prepare a memoir on my examples. This, when done, was published in the fourth volume of the third series of Memoirs of the Literary and Philosophical Society of Manchester.

But, before referring further to the views advanced in that memoir, a much larger question requires to be considered, viz., the amount of knowledge which the geologist had attained to respecting the plants of the carboniferous age.

A considerable number of writers in various parts of the world had already called attention to a limited number of isolated facts bearing on the subject, but these facts were as yet too few to make broad and philosophical conclusions on the matter possible.

Nothing being known of the specimens which these earlier authors described, beyond the external forms of isolated fragments, conclusions of any value respecting their relation to living plants were out of the question. At length, however, the time and the man arrived, when the attempt was made.

A son of Alexander Brongniart, the eminent French geologist, turned his attention not only to recent botany, but to the fossil forms of plant life. At a very early age he succeeded in bringing together a large collection of fossil plants, which he studied with the utmost care, and in 1828 he issued a " Prodrome d'une Histoire des Végétaux Fossiles," in which he announced a forthcoming work on a large scale, to be entitled, " Histoire des Végétaux Fossiles, " ou Recherches Botaniques et Geologiques sur les " Végétaux Renfermés dans les Diverses Couches " du Globe."

This work was intended to constitute two quarto volumes, to appear in from twenty to thirty parts, with from 180 to 200 plates. It was to be devoted partly to a description of the genera and species of fossil plants, and partly to a study of their relations to living plants.

Though the " Prodrome " inevitably abounded in errors, it gave us for the first time a philosophic arrangement of the classes, families, and genera of fossil plants then known, in four successive periods of the earth's past history. It would have been better had he adhered to this classification, because it was far more accurate than others which he substituted at later periods of his life. The larger quarto work was never completed. The first volume appeared as well as one or two parts of the second. He showed that nearly all the plants living at the most ancient geological epochs were Cryptogams, chiefly belonging to the great families of the Ferns, the Equiseta, and the Lycopods, or club mosses ; but that whilst most of those living now are small herbaceous objects, during the carboniferous age they were magnificent forest trees, whilst none of the modern denizens of our forests were to be found among them. Of these ancient Cryptogams he described 225 species, whilst in the entire range of rocks he discovered about twenty-six that could be regarded as representatives of the flowering plants, and in twenty of these he was certainly mistaken. Nevertheless, the above was a grand generalisation, which, to a large extent, continues to be true, notwithstanding the gigantic progress of research during the last seventy years. No wonder that its author at once took the position he so well deserved, of the foremost palæo-botanist of the age.

Unhappily Brongniart was the first to strike a serious blow at his own philosophy. During his earlier years nothing was known of the internal organisation of these fossil plants. We had nothing beyond their external forms to guide us as to their position in nature's scale.

Many years later two specimens fell into Brongniart's hands, one an equisetiform Calamite, and the other a lycopodiaceous Sigillaria, in each of which the internal structure was preserved. In one of these plants was found a central pith surrounded by an exogenously developed cylinder of wood. In the Sigillaria a similar condition existed. These woody zones were unquestionably formed by true cambium layers. Brongniart then believed that no living Cryptogam possessed a cambium; hence he concluded that both the Calamite and the Sigillaria must be removed from the positions in which he had originally placed them amongst the Cryptogams, and he classed them both with the Conifers and Cycads, believing them to be gymnospermous plants. This error has led to nearly thirty years of conflict amongst palæo-botanists.

In 1832 a new specimen was obtained by the late William Vernon Harcourt, of York. It was a fragment of a branch of a Lepidodendron, a lycopodiaceous genus, in which much of the internal organisation was beautifully preserved. After being described in England, first by Mr. Witham, of Lartington, and subsequently by the authors of the " Fossil Flora of Great Britain," a section of it was obtained by M. Brongniart, and carefully described by him. This was one of those Lepidodendra which do not develop their woody cylinder until an advanced period of growth. Hence, notwithstanding the many existing features of close identity between Sigillaria and Lepidodendron, Brong-

niart now adopted the opinion that Lepidodendron
was a cryptogamic Lycopod, because it did not pos-
sess a woody cylinder, but that Sigillaria was a
Gymnosperm because it did.   Even in his valuable
"Tableaux des Genres de Végétaux Fossiles," published in 1849, he still clung to his mistaken notions
respecting these plants.

Up to this time I did not know where Mr. Binney
had got his specimens, but I soon had the advantage of
an introduction to Mr. J. Butterworth of Shaw, near
Oldham, who had not only collected plants from the
localities which had supplied Mr. Binney with his,
but had fitted up an excellent lapidary's lathe and
prepared some sections of the fossil plants, of which
he showed me a small but beautiful series.   He also
supplied me with a number of the hard calcareous
nodules dug out of the coal, from which these plants,
the internal tissues of which were so beautifully
preserved, were obtained.   I at once provided myself
with a jeweller's lathe, and commenced that series of
practical researches which have continued until now.
After devoting some time to the practical manipula-
tion of my machine, I became sufficiently accustomed
to the work to produce very respectable and instructive sections.

I first directed my attention to the Calamitean
problem, and soon obtained a very important series
of these objects in addition to some lent to me by
Mr. Butterworth.   On comparing these with Brongniart's, and with those of Mr. Binney, I found myself

unable to agree with either of them.   I then formed
a resolution which has been of the greatest service
to me.   Remembering how I had been misled in my
earliest researches amongst the Foraminifera by
relying upon the authority of M. Ehrenberg, I determined not to look at the writings of any other
observer until I had studied every specimen in my
cabinet, and arrived at my own conclusions as to
what they taught.

Having thus formed my own independent judg-
ment, I then turned to the works of other writers on
the same subjects to learn in detail what their views
were.   Dealing with the Calamites on this plan, I
found that I was the possessor of a mass of entirely
new facts.   These I determined ere long to repro-
duce in an illustrated memoir.

Mr. Butterworth gave me a section from a specimen which he had picked up, and which I at once
saw had a great interest; but his kindness did not
stop here.   On examining the fragment not yet cut
up, we determined upon the direction in which
further sections could advantageously be made, and
which he undertook to make for me.

Mr. Butterworth being at that time an overlooker
in a large cotton mill, was eminently skilled in
matters relating to machinery.

When the sections just referred to were all prepared I made them the subject of a second memoir,
entitled: "On a New Form of Calamitean Strobilus
"from the Lancashire Coal Measures."   This memoir

was printed in the fourth volume of the third series of the " Memoirs of the Literary and Philosophical " Society of Manchester," session 1869–70. Though it could not be proved that this strobilus was actually a fructification of a Calamite, it presented too many features of identity to leave any doubt on my own mind that such was the case. But specimens of the object were extremely rare, and nearly twenty years had to elapse before additional examples were obtained, which demonstrated the correctness of my original conclusion.

In November 1870 I sent in to the Royal Society my first memoir " On the Organisation of the Fossil " Plants of the Coal Measures "—Part I. Calamites. In a few days I received a note from the secretary, then my old friend Professor Sharpey, asking me to withdraw the expression Part I., since it bound the Society to publish Part II. at some subsequent time. I declined to do so, because I knew that a number of parts would have to be published before the materials already in hand were exhausted.

I heard nothing further of the matter, and was in ignorance about what followed, until, at a much later date, I was told by the late Professor Duncan, the well-known geologist, that the referees, animated by the same spirit as the rest of the palæo-botanical world, had recommended that the paper should not be published ; but that there were others on the Council who had too much confidence in me to accept that decree, and through their resolution the memoir was ordered by the Council to be printed. This memoir contained an outline of my views respecting Brongniart. A second memoir was read in 1871 and published in 1872, and when the sixth memoir was read in 1874 the Royal Society, then presided over by Sir Joseph Hooker, rewarded my heresies by voting to me one of their gold medals.

In August of 1871, the year in which my memoir on Calamites was published in the *Philosophical Transactions*, the British Association met at Edinburgh. At that meeting I brought forward the subject of cambiums and secondary woods in Cryptogams, with the result that my views were rejected by every botanist in the room. On my return home I found myself in September and October drawn into a controversy on the same subject in the pages of *Nature*, where the seriousness of the errors into which I had fallen was demonstrated by my opponents, especially by Professor McNab. But in the number for October 26, the editor wisely closed the discussion, on the ground that I should be allowed to publish my new facts. This was done, and a few years later, I had nowhere a stronger supporter than the same Professor McNab.

The fight was always the same: Was Brongniart right or wrong, when he uttered his dogma, that if the stem of a fossil plant contained a secondary growth of wood, the product of a cambium layer, it could not possibly belong to the cryptogamic division of the vegetable kingdom ? Three palæo-botanists

resided in France who had personally been pupils of
Brongniart, whose utterances were in their minds
infallible and unassailable. One of these was M.
Renault, of the Geological Museum of the Jardin
des Plantes at Paris, in whose care Brongniart's
collection of fossil plants was placed. The second
was my friend M. Grand' Eury, then a young but
extremely able and energetic mining engineer, who
resided at St. Etienne, in the middle of one of the
most important of the coal-producing districts of
Central France. The third was the Marquis
de Saporta, a descendant of the old French noblesse,
who had been robbed of his ancestral possessions
during the Revolution, but who at a later period had
recovered some property and still resided in the
family château at Aix, in Provence. Each of these
observers was a voluminous writer, and their most
important works, especially those of MM. Renault
and Grand' Eury were in connection with the vegetation of the carboniferous age. The consequence
was that most of their writings teemed with attacks
upon the views that I was promulgating. Being in
friendly correspondence with all of them, I paid
little attention to their aggressive utterances, but
steadily persevered in my investigations, the results
of which were chiefly published in volume after
volume of the *Philosophical Transactions*, between
1872 and the present time, but now and then I fired
a broadside into the enemy's camp. At that time my
friend Professor Hartog of Queen's College, Cork,

was my demonstrator at the Owens College, and, assured of the advantage of his friendly co-operation, I wrote to M. Van Tieghem, inquiring whether if I sent him a French controversial article dealing with these attacks upon my views by my French friends, he would publish it in the *Annales des Sciences Naturelles*, of which he was then the editor. He promptly replied that he would publish whatever I chose to send him.

Thus encouraged, I prepared with the utmost care a review of the positions taken up, more especially by M. Renault, and replied to them seriatim. I placed this manuscript in the hands of Mr. Hartog, who translated it into French. My memoir was flung like a bombshell amongst my opponents. In it I called upon palæo-botanists of other parts of Europe to take note of my contradictions of many of M. Renault's statements, and of my assertions that our British specimens of carboniferous plants differed absolutely from many of M. Renault's descriptions of the French ones.

In all such controversies time is an important element. Those who conscientiously hold opposing views on such questions cannot be expected at once to haul down their flags ; they need time to consider and measure the value of facts and arguments advanced by their opponents ; and so it happened in the present instance. The two prominent fossil plants which were the subjects of discussion were the Calamites and the Sigillariæ. This demonstration.

of my views was made somewhere about 1883 ; their
first acceptance in France was by M. Zeiller of the
Paris School of Mines. He had fortunately obtained
a fructification of a true Sigillaria which was unquestionably cryptogamic in every feature, hence he
announced his recognition of my views. Still later
I received a letter from M. Grand' Eury expressing
his new conviction that I was right in placing my
Calamites amongst the Cryptogams, and in May 27,
1889, he sent to the Institute a brief notice to that
effect, which was published in the *Comptes Rendus
des Sciences.* One result of M. Zeiller's memoir
was that in 1885 M. Renault, the most determined
of my opponents, and most devoted supporter of the
Brongniartian school, felt compelled to make the following admission: " Les Sigillaires groupe de plantes,
" essentiellement de transition, se diviseraient alors
" en *Leiodermariées* on *Sigillaires phanérogames* à
" écorce lisse, voisines des Cycadées, et Rhytidolepcés
"ou *Sigillaires cryptogames,* à ecorce cannelée, voisines
" des Isoëtes," December 7, 1885, *Comptes Rendus des
Séances de l'Academie des Sciences.*

This was a large admission in favour of the views
for which I had then been contending for fifteen or
sixteen years ; the more so because even then
the Leiodermariæ constituted but an unimportant
division of the Sigillariæ, and did not include those
forms upon which Brongniart had based his views.
At a later period this division was practically thrown
overboard, because examples of stems were found

which were Leiodermarian on one side and not so
on the opposite one.

In 1890 M. Grand' Eury issued his noble work,
" Géologie et Palæontologie du Bassin Houiller du
" Gard." On his first page he says, " Autrefois, on
" ne connaissait pas des cryptogames à structure
" rayonnante et l'analogie forcait d'admettre que
" tous les végétaux ainsi organisés se rangent parmi
" les Gymnospermes. Aujourd'hui qu'on a trouvé
" un reste de bois centrifuge dans les Ophioglossums,
" et que M. Williamson a découvert du bois exogène
" dans le Lepidodendron selaginoides, la question a
" changé de face. M. Williamson après vingt années
" d'études anatomiques sur les végétaux fossiles
" calcifies du Lancashire et de Burntisland, estime
" que la structure des tiges de Diploxylon est l'apanage
" des cryptogames primitives." " En tout cas
" l'opinion que les Sigillaires et les Calamodendrons
" sont des Gymnospermes voit de jour en jour le
" nombre de ses adeptes diminuer. A la suite de
" mes études dans le Gard, j'ai été amené à les
" tenir pour des cryptogames, hautement organisées."
Precisely the view for which I fought ; but when so
distinguished and experienced a man as M. Grand'
Eury honourably and decidedly abandoned opinions
for which he had contended ·long and stoutly, he not
only showed the world how true and unselfish a man
of science he was, but how futile would be the efforts
of smaller men to put backward the hands of the
scientific clock. The contest, so far as this great

question of the existence of an active cambium zone producing secondary wood in the stem of the Crypto-gams is concerned, was settled for ever.

My chief remaining opponent the Marquis de Saporta, having relied upon men like Grand' Eury for his facts in this controversy, gave way at once when these supports were withdrawn.

For many years I failed to discover any plants of the class of Ferns that possessed this exogenous organisation, though I had in my cabinet specimens of the genus Lyginodendron, which I strongly suspected of belonging to that group. It required twenty years of vigilant research before I obtained, in 1892, unquestionable proof that my suspicions were correct, and that my plant, which, along with two or three congeners, exhibits some of the finest exogenous structures that I have found in these ancient beds, really belongs to the Ferns of that primeval age.*

* Dr. Williamson had always intended writing some account of the men to whose untiring zeal and keen observation he was indebted for the material which gave rise to his long series of Memoirs on Fossil Plants. He was prevented by failing health from doing what he wished ; but after his death, I found a paper, the last he touched, with the following names in pencil : " Butter-worth, Whitaker, Binns, G. Wilde, Earnshaw, Spencer, Nield, Hemmingway, Lomax." Excepting a few speci-mens given to him by friends and fellow-workers, these men furnished all he possessed. The cabinet containing them has been purchased by the British Museum, and is now in the Natural History Department, South Kensington.

CHAPTER XIV

From 1887 to the End

[Continuation by Mrs. WILLIAMSON]

DR. WILLIAMSON and I spent our holiday, after the close of the British Association meeting, at Scarborough, where we had never been together without visiting some of his old haunts.

This year we went to all of them ; to the spot on which he was born, now changed, of course ; to the cottage where he had droned his A B C; to the district that had yielded his largest supply of insects ; to Mr. Potter's school. We went to the Lebberston farm cottage, where he had spent so many summers, and we wandered over fields in which he had spouted poetry to frighten the crows. We stood at the Thornton desk, where he had shed bitter tears over his Latin grammar, and we picniced under his favourite nesting trees.

To the Museum he never tired of going ; he almost embraced the brown old skeleton that had inspired one of his earliest papers, and he not only knew every bird in the place, but could give vivid accounts of the killing and stuffing of most of them. We lingered in the glorious bays that he had roamed with gun or hammer, and we rounded the great cliffs to the perpendicular glory of which he was accustomed, but which almost stunned me. He stepped over the slippery, fossil-strewn beach, like an old war-horse roused by the long forgotten sound of his trumpet. Indeed, he seemed through these weeks in almost everything a boy again ; and I have wondered since if he felt at all that this might be his last look of the beauties he loved so dearly. He was so fresh and bright and joyous that no thought of the kind spoiled my pleasure. Our last day was spent at Hackness, in the home of his old schoolfellow and lifelong friend, Mr. Robert Turnbull.

Still, this summer of '87 was only a flicker, and, as it proved, the last flicker of health. His strength had been a good deal undermined by an attack of diabetes in '83 and '84, and it now steadily declined. A couple of years later, as we were riding up the " Engstlen Alp," in the Oberland, one of the horses kicked his shin. He suffered a good deal, notwithstanding the daily care of Dr. Bardeleben, Surgeon General of the German Army, who happened to be in the same little chalet, indeed he was disabled for the whole of our visit ; and we suspected the prostration arose more from previous over-fatigue than from the wound.

Though during the following winter, lectures, classes, and even his garden gave more fatigue than pleasure, it was not until the close of a happy stay in Scotland that I became seriously anxious.

During a small impromptu concert he suddenly fainted, and the faint was long and severe. Immediately on our return home I asked the help of my husband's old friend, Dr. Hecksher, who had attended him through the severe illness of thirty years before, and who knew his constitution thoroughly well.

Dr. Hecksher, after careful examination, found nothing worse than the effect of overwork, showing itself in what he called "deterioration." Dr. Williamson had given up medical practice some time before; he now discontinued popular lectures, though the loss cost him a wrench, as he intensely enjoyed this part of his work, and we practically ceased visiting. With these reductions the winter passed fairly well, but the summer again tried him severely, and in an hotel in Geneva he had another serious faint.

He had spent an afternoon with his old friend and fellow botanist, M. de Candolle, to the mutual enjoyment of the veterans. After this visit he joined us full of pleasures already enjoyed, and of plans for the morrow.

In the morning he looked tired and unwell, but preferred to come downstairs for breakfast, still before coffee appeared, he became so much more strange, I urged his lying down. He walked with help to the door of the room and then fell. We took him upstairs, and after perfect quiet for a day or two he was sufficiently recovered to travel, though the journey home was slow and painful. M. Casimir de Candolle, son of the venerable botanist, came to the hotel immediately after my husband's attack with the hope of showing us special sights in Geneva, and did for us everything possible to prevent our feeling of helplessness in a strange town.

Once home, Dr. Hecksher came to the rescue and again urged a decrease of work. But how to reduce it further was the difficulty. Dr. Williamson loved his winter class and his evening class; these did him no harm; but although the college council granted him as much extra help as he asked, and in spite of the capable and devoted efforts of his friend and demonstrator, Mr. Hicks, the influx of medical students for the summer class was the crux. Neither Dr. Hecksher nor I thought he could muster strength for another struggle.

My husband's children joined me in definitely facing the problem, and in trying to determine what steps should be taken to avert a breakdown. We were afraid of reducing work too much, as this would bring evils worse than those we were trying to escape; and he very much dreaded any further serious reduction of income. Still, after a careful survey of the position, Dr. Hecksher, his children and myself agreed, that the inevitable step was the resignation of his Chair of Botany.

He would then be able to continue all research work, and this would give him unending interest.

Considering his forty-one years of unbroken service for Owens College, he thought himself entitled to a pension and asked for one. The Council refused, because of their fear of creating a precedent. This refusal took away a long-indulged anticipation of spending his last winters in the South of Europe, but his private purse enabled us to live quietly in a London suburb.

He always appeared to, and I think he honestly did, enjoy the change. Many of his oldest and nearly all his scientific friends were already in London. He had the pleasure of regularly attending meetings of the Royal Society, and he was pleased with the enthusiastic reception accorded him by the several Natural Science Societies of the metropolis. Though, after leaving the North, he never touched pencil, for either landscape or scientific drawing, he continued to employ himself in investigations of carboniferous flora.

His great wish had been to find some young, eager botanist who would take up and continue this work. He succeeded in persuading Dr. Dukenfield Scott, F.R.S., honorary keeper of the Joddrell laboratories at Kew, to take an interest in it.

To Dr. Scott's intellectual enthusiasm for the subject, to his tactful veneration for its exponent, and to his unfailing kindness, my husband owed much of the enjoyment of his last years.

The distinctly marked downward steps had in each case been an attack of unconsciousness. Toward the end of January, 1895, he suffered from one worse than any before. The Christmas had been a singularly happy one, all his own children and many of my people had been about us ; perhaps the strength had been once more overtaxed, and for nearly five months he was invalided.

He still retained interest in passing events. During the latter half of April he was able to drive and even walk a little. He went once to a meeting of the Royal Society, Dr. Scott was guardian ; and when the tired, nervous face became overstrained, he fabricated some excuse for bringing his friend away.

The invalid was enthusiastically interested in the School Boards, and on election day was sufficiently well to be driven in the carriage of sympathetic friends to the polling booth ; for the hour he looked brisk, and young, and full of life.

After this, one or two walks on Clapham Common, and the last one to the garden of a nurseryman who had had some favourite plants in charge for the winter ; he grew tired on the way home, and we drove, but he came into his house a little saddened.

During May and part of June he was confined to his room ; even still he loved to be surrounded by his children and a few intimate friends, and the tea-table upstairs was almost as often cheered by the presence of some bright visitor as the table downstairs had been.

But his powers waned steadily, the last and most touching loss being that of sight. I do not think he

ever understood his blindness, but the pathetic movement of the hand to adjust his spectacles showed he
knew something was wrong.

To within a few minutes of the end he recognised
my touch, and responded with a hand clasp.

We watched him, his eldest daughter, our son,
and I, through the long dawn of a beautiful June
morning. About five he fell asleep, as a child
might, his vast individuality living still, an inspira-
tion to those who loved him.

APPROXIMATE LIST OF WRITINGS BY
DR. W. C. WILLIAMSON

A Notice of Localities, Habits, Characteristics, and Synonyms of a Rare British Species of Mytilus. *Magazine of Natural History.* VII. 1834.

On the Distribution of Organic Remains in the Lias Series of Yorkshire, with a view to facilitate its Identification, by giving the Situation of its Fossils, 1834. *Geological Society's Proceedings.* II. 1833–1838.

Description of the Tumulus lately opened at Gristhorpe near Scarborough, 1834.

Second Edition, 1835.

Illustrations and Descriptions for the Fossil Flora of Great Britain. Lindley and Hutton, 1835.

On the Distribution of Organic Remains in the Oolitic Formations of the Yorkshire Coast, 1836. *Geological Society's Proceedings.* II. 1833–38.

On the Distribution of Organic Remains in part of the Oolitic Series on the Coast of Yorkshire. *Geological Society's Proceedings.* II.

A Notice of a hitherto Undescribed Species of Radiara, from the Marlstone of Yorkshire, and Remarks on the Organic Remains in that Stratum. *Magazine of Natural History.* IX. 1836.

On the Limestones found in the vicinity of Manchester. *Philosophical Magazine.* London & Edinburgh. IX. 1836.

Notes on the Appearance of Rare Birds in the vicinity of Scarborough. *Proceedings of the Zoological Society.* IV. 1836.

On Fossil Fishes in the Lancashire Coal Fields, 1837. *Geological Society's Proceedings.* II.

On the Affinity of some Fossil Scales of Fish from the Lancashire Coal Measures, with those of the recent Salmonidæ. *Philosophical Magizine.* XI. 1837.

Section of the Carboniferous Strata of Western Lancashire from its highest beds at Ardwick, down nearly to the Millstone Grit. *British Association.* Liverpool, 1837.

On the Distribution of Organic Remains in the Strata of the Yorkshire Coast from the Upper Sandstone to the Oxford Clay, inclusive, 1838. *Geological Society's Proceedings.* VI. 1842.

On the Fossil Fishes of the Yorkshire and Lancashire Coalfields. *Geological Society's Proceedings.* III. 1839.

On the Distribution of Fossil Remains on the Yorkshire Coast, from the Lower Lias to the Bath Oolite, inclusive. *Geological Society's Proceedings.* V. 1840.

On some Geological Specimens from Syria. *Geological Society's Proceedings.* III. 1840.

On the Origin of Coal. *British Association Report,* 1842.

On some Microscopical Objects found in the Mud of the Levant and other Deposits, with Remarks on the Mode of Formation of Calcareous and Infusorial Siliceous Rocks. 1845. *Manchester Philosophical Society's Memoirs.* VIII.

On the Real Nature of the Minute Bodies in Flints, supposed to be Sponge Spiculæ. 1846. *Annals Natural History*. XVII.

On the Recent British Species of the Genus Lagena. 1848. *Annals Natural History*. I.

On a New British Species of Campylodiscus. 1848. *Annals Natural History*.

On the Structure of the Shell and Soft Animal of the Polystomella Crispa. With some Remarks on the Zoological Position of the Foraminifera. 1848. *Microscopical Society's Transactions*. II.

On the Microscopic Structure of the Scales and Dermal Teeth of some Ganoid and Placoid Fishes. 1849. *Philosophical Transactions of the Royal Society of London*.

Investigations into the Structure and Development of the Scales and Bones of Fishes. 1850. *Philosophical Society's Transactions*. 1851.

On the Minute Structure of the Calcareous Shells of some recent Species of Foraminifera. 1850. *Microscopical Society's Transactions*. III.

On the Volvox Globator. 1851. *Manchester Philosophical Society's Memoirs*. IX.

On the Structure and Affinities of the Plants hitherto known as Sternbergiæ. 1851. *Manchester Philosophical Society's Memoirs*. IX.

On the Minute Structure of a Species of Fanjasina. *Microscopical Society's Transactions*. 1851.

On the Study of Natural History. 1851. Introductory Lecture at Owens College, Manchester.

Further Elucidations of the Structure of Volvox Globator. 1852. *Microscopical Society's Transactions*. I.

On the Anatomy of Melecerta Ringens. 1853. *Journal Microscopic Science*. I.

On the Restoration of *Zamia gigas* from the Lower Sand-stone and Shale of the Yorkshire Coast. *British Association Report*. 1854.

On the Scaly Vegetable Heads or Collars from Runswick Bay, supposed to belong to *Zamia gigas*. *Yorkshire Philosopical Society's Proceedings*. 1855.

On the Histology of Dental and Allied Dermal Tissues of Vertebrate and Invertebrate Animals. Parts I. II. 1856–57. *British Journal of Dental Science*.

Enlargement of the Tonsil and Uvula in relation to Deafness. *British Medical Journal*, 1857.

On the Prolonged Use of Chloroform in a Case of Infantile Convulsions. *British Medical Journal*.

On some Difficulties encountered in the Diagnosis of Aural Diseases.

Inaugural Address to the Microscopic Section of the Manchester Literary and Philosophical Society. 1859.

On the Recent Foraminifera of Great Britain. *Ray Society*. 1858.

The Amœba, its Structure and Development.
The Common Fresh Water Sponge

On some Histological Features in the Shell of the Crustacea. 1860. *Journal of Microscopic Science*,

Papers written for the *London Quarterly Review* :
On the British Association for the Advancement of Science.
The Natural History of Man.
Animal Organisation.
Reports of the Registrar-General.
Anatomical Science, its History and Progress.
Progress of Modern Geology.
Brazil and the Amazon.

Papers written for the *London Quarterly Review*—continued :
  Cryptogamic Vegetation.
  Michael Faraday.
  Floriculture.
  Life in the Deep Seas.
  Ancient Vegetation.
  Geology of the Drift.
  Professor Edward Forbes.
  Revelations of the Microscope.

On the Anatomy and Physiology of the Foraminifera. *Popular Science Review*, 1865.

On the Anatomy and Affinities of some Exogenous Stems of the Coal Measures. *Monthly Microscopical Journal*, 1869.

On a Cheirotherian Footprint from the Base of the Keuper Sandstone of Daresbury, Cheshire. *Geological Society's Proceedings*, 1866.

On the Structure of an Undescribed Type of Calamodendron from the Upper Coal Measures of Lancashire. *Manchester Literary and Philosophical Society's Proceedings*, VIII. 1868.

Contributions towards the History of Zamia gigas, Lindley and Hutton. *Linnean Society's Transactions.* 1868. XXVI.

Additional Notes on the Structure of Calamites. *Manchester Literary and Philosophical Society's Proceedings.* VIII. 1869.

On the Structure and Affinities of some Exogenous Stems from the Coal Measures. 1869. *Monthly Microscopical Journal.* II.

What is Bathybius? *Popular Science Review.* VIII. 1869.

On the Organisation of the Stems of Calamites. *British Association Report.* 1870. *Manchester Literary and Philosophical Society's Proceedings.* IX. 1870.

On a New Form of Calamitean Strobilus. 1869. *Manchester Literary and Philosophical Society's Proceedings.* IX. 1870. *Manchester Literary and Philosophical Society's Memoirs.* IV. 1871.

On the Structure of the Gizzards and Teeth of Rotifera. *Manchester Literary and Philosophical Society's Proceedings.* IX. 1870.

On the Sphærosira Volvox, Ehrenb. *Popular Science Review.* IX. 1870.

On the Structure of the Dictyoxylons of the Coal Measures.

On the Classification of the Vascular Cryptogamia, as affected by Recent Discoveries amongst the Fossil Plants of the Coal Measures. *British Association Report.* XLI. 1871.

On the Structure of the Woody Zone of an Undescribed form of Calamite (? Calamopitus). 1868. *Manchester Literary and Philosophical Society's Memoirs.* IV. 1871.

On the Organisation of an Undescribed Verticillate Strobilus from the Lower Coal Measures of Lancashire. *Manchester Literary and Philosophical Society's Proceedings.* X. 1871.

On the Structure of some Specimens of Stigmaria. *Manchester Literary and Philosophical Society's Proceedings.* X. 1871.

Exogenous Structures among the Stems of the Coal Measures. *Nature.* IV. 1871.

On the Organisation of Volkmania Dawsoni. *Manchester Literary and Philosopical Society.* 1871.

On the Organisation of the Fossil Plants of the Coal Measures. Part I. Calamites. 1870. *Philosophical Society Transactions.* CLXI. 1871. *Annals and Magazine Natural History.* VII. 1871.

Part II. Lycopodiaceæ, Lepidodendra, and Sigillariæ, with Supplementary Observations. 1871. *Philosophical Transactions.* CLXII. 1872. *Royal Society's Proceedings.* XIX. 1871. *Annals and Magazine Natural History.* VIII. 1871.

Part III. Lycopodiaceæ. *Philosophical Transactions.* CLXII. 1872. *Royal Society's Proceedings.* X. 1872.

Part IV. Dictyoxylon, Lyginodendron, and Heterangium. *Philosophical Transactions.* CLXIII. 1873. *Royal Society's Proceedings.* XXI. 1873.

Part V. Asterophyllites. *Philosophical Transactions.* CLXIV. 1874. *Royal Society's Proceedings.* XXI. 1873. *Monthly Microscopical Journal.* X. 1873.

Part VI. Ferns. *Philosophical Transactions.* CLXIV. 1874. *Royal Society's Proceedings.* XXII. 1874.

Part VII. Myelopteris, Psaronius, and Kaloxylon. 1875. *Philosophical Transactions.* CLXVI. 1877. *Royal Society's Proceedings.* 1875.

Part VIII. Ferns continued, and Gymnospermous Stems and Seeds. 1876. *Philosophical Transactions.* 1878. *Royal Society's Proceedings.* XXV. 1877. *Annals and Magazine Natural History.* 1876.

Part IX. The Bakerian Lecture. On Latest Researches into the Organisation of the Fossil Plants of the British Coal Measures, especially of the Calamites and Lepidodendra. 1877. *Philosophical Transactions.* CLXIX. 1879. *Royal Society's Proceedings.* XXVI. 1878.

Part X. (Including an Examination of the Supposed Radiolarians of the Carboniferous Rocks.) 1879. *Philosophical Transactions.* ·1881. *Royal Society's Proceedings.* XXVIII. 1879.

Part XI. 1880. *Philosophical Transactions.* CLXXII. 1882. *Royal Society's Proceedings.* XXX. 1880. *Nature.* XXII. 1880.

Part XII. 1882. *Philosophical Transactions.* CLXXIV. 1884.

Part XIII. Heterangium Tiliæoides (Williamson), and Kaloxylon Hookeri. 1886. *Philosophical Transactions.* 1887.

Part XIV. The True Fructification of Calamites. 1887. *Philosophical Transactions.* 1888.

Part XV. 1888. *Philosophical Transactions.* 1889.

Part XVI. 1889. *Philosophical Transactions.* 1889.

Part XVII. Lyginodendron Oldhamium and Rachiopteris aspera. 1890. *Philosophical Transactions.* 1890.

Part XVIII. 1891. *Philosophical Transactions.* 1891.

Part XIX. 1892. *Philosophical Transactions.* 1893.

On Coal and Coal Plants. *Macmillan's Magazine.* 1873.

On the Structure of Stigmaria. 1874. *Manchester Literary and Philosophical Society's Proceedings.* XIV. 1875. *Nature.* XI. 1875.

Primeval Vegetation in its Relation to the Doctrines of Natural Selection and Evolution. 1874. Lecture at Owens College. Macmillan & Co.

La Végétation Primitive dans ses Rapports avec la Sélection Naturelle et la Théorie de l'Évolution. *Revue Scientifique.* VIII. 1875.

On some Fossil Seeds from the Lower Carboniferous Beds of Lancashire. *British Association Report.* 1875.

Corrections of the Nomenclature of the Objects Figured in a Memoir "On some of the Minute Objects found in the Mud of the Levant." 1872. *Manchester Literary and Philosophical Society.* Memoir V. 1876.

Recent Researches into the Organisation of some of the Plants of the Coal Measures. On some Physiological and Morphological Features seen in the Plants of the Coal Measures. *British Association Report.* 1876.

Reminiscences of a Yorkshire Naturalist. Three Papers for *Good Words*. 1877.

Microscopic Conditions of a Slab of Mountain Limestone of Bolland. *Manchester Literary and Philosophical Society*. 1878.

On the Supposed Radiolarians and Diatoms of the Carboniferous Rocks. *British Association Report*. 1878.

On the Botanical Affinities of the Carboniferous Sigillariæ. *British Association Report*. 1879.

Sphenophyllum, Asterophyllites und Calamites deren Stellung zu Einander Nach den letzten Beobachtungen. *Neues Jahrb. Mineral*. 1879. *Nature*. XX. 1879.

The Natural History of Paving Stones. 1871. Earthquakes and Volcanoes. 1874. Insectivorous Plants. 1878. Science Lectures for the People. John Heywood, Manchester.

Dawn of Animal Life. 1875. Coals and Coal Plants. 1875. The Ice Age. 1877. *Glasgow Science Lecture Association*.

Succession of Life on the Earth. 1876. Manchester Science Lectures for the People. Macmillan & Co.

Preliminary Remarks on the Microscopic Structure of Coal. *British Association Report*. 1881.

The Evolution of the Palæozoic Vegetation. *Nature*. 1881.

Helophyton Williamsonis. 1881. *Nature*. 1882.

On the Morphology of the Pitcher of Cephalotus Follicularis. *Nature*. 1883.

Presidential Address to the Geological Section of the British Association at Southport. 1883 The Present State of our Knowledge of the Vegetation of the Carboniferous Age. *British Association Report.* 1883. *Nature.* 1883.

On some Anomalous Oolitic and Palæozoic Forms of Vegetation. 1883. *Royal Institution Proceedings.* 1884.

Williamson and Hartog. Les Sigillaires et les Lepidodendrées. *Annales des Sciences Naturelles (Botanique).* 1882.

On Pyrrhonism in Science. *Contemporary Review.* 1881.

Biographical Notice of an Eminent Yorkshire Geologist, John Williamson. *Geological and Polytechnic Society of the West Riding of Yorkshire.* 1883.

On some Undescribed Tracks of Invertebrate Animals from the Carboniferous Rocks; and on some Inorganic Phenomena Simulating Plant Remains Produced on Tidal Shores. *Literary and Philosophical Society, Manchester.* 1885.

Address at Owens College. *Manchester Geological Society.* 1885.

On Heterangium tiliæoides and Kaloxylon Hookeri. *Proceedings Royal Society.* 1886.

Note on Lepidodendron Harcourtii and Lepidodendron Fuliginosum. *Proceedings Royal Society.* 1886.

On the Morphology of Pinites Oblongus. *Manchester Literary and Philosophical Society.* 1886.

On the True Fructification of Carboniferous Calamites. *Proceedings Royal Society.* 1887.

On the Relation of Calamodendron to Calamites. *Manchester Literary and Philosophical Society.* 1887.

Preliminary Report of the Committee, consisting of W. C. Williamson and Mr. Wm. Cash, F.G.S., on the Flora of the Halifax Hard Bed. *British Association.* 1886.

Report of the above Committee. 1887.

Monograph on the Morphology and Histology of Stigmaria Ficoides. *Palæontographical Society.* 1887.

On Goethe as Botanist and Osteologist. Publications of the *English Goethe Society.* 1887.

On the Fossil Trees of the Coal Measures. *Manchester Geological Society.* 1888.

On some Anomalous Cells developed within the Interior of the Vascular and Cellular Tissues of the Fossil Plants of the Coal Measures. *Annals of Botany.* 1888.

General Morphological and Histological Index to the Author's Collective Memoirs on the Fossil Plants of the Coal Measures. Introduction, 1890. Part I., 1891. Part II., 1893. Part III., 1894. *Manchester Literary and Philosophical Society's Proceedings.*

On our Present Knowledge of the Vegetation of the Carboniferous Age and the Further Advancement of the Study of the Subject. *Manchester Geological Society.* 1891.

Earlier Palæontographical Work. *Manchester Geological Society.* 1892.

Is Stigmaria a Root or a Rhizome? *Natural Science.* Macmillan & Co. 1892.

Sigillaria and Stigmaria. By Sir William Dawson and W. C. Williamson. *Natural Science.* Macmillan & Co. 1892.

The Genus Sphenophyllum. *Nature.* 1892.

Address on the Mineralisation of Minute Tissues of Animals and Plants. *Journal of the Quekett Microscopic Club.* 1893.

Corrections of an Error in Part XIX. of the Author's Memoirs on the Organisation of the Fossil Plants of the Coal Measures. *Proceedings Royal Society.* 1894.

On Light thrown upon the Question of the Growth and Development of the Carboniferous Arborescent Lepidodendra, by a Study of the Details of their Organisation. *Manchester Literary and Philosophical Society.* 1894.

Obituary Notice of Le Marquis Gaston de Saporta. *Manchester Literary and Philosophical Society.* 1896.

Further Observations on the Organisation of the Fossil Plants of the Coal Measures. [In collaboration with Dr. D. H. Scott.]

Part I. Calamites, Calamostachys and Sphenophyllum. 1893. *Philosophical Transactions.* 1895.

Part II. The Roots of Calamites. 1894. *Philosophical Transactions.* 1895.

Part III. Lyginodendron and Heterangium. 1895. *Philosophical Transactions.*

Printed by BALLANTYNE, HANSON & Co.
London and Edinburgh

www.ingramcontent.com/pod-product-compliance
Lightning Source LLC
Chambersburg PA
CBHW022000050726
47498CB00006BA/2090